Ricki's Road to Redemption

Ricki's Road to Redemption

As told to Shapoor Batliwalla

ISBN 13: 978-93-90507-72-6
ISBN 10: 93-90507-72-3

Printed in India and published by BUUKS.

To an incredible land
Where nothing works
Yet everything always works out.

TABLE OF CONTENTS

OPENING CREDITS

Even before I met the gentleman to whom this story belongs, I was determined not to like him. Having hung up on him several times, I thought I might have heard the last of him.

Not so.

One afternoon, I was summoned to meet him in a manner I could not refuse; two large men, who would not take no for an answer, camped at my door.

I had, up to this moment, refused his entreaties because I was quite sure that he, as with other men who believed their lives were fascinating enough for the world to want to read about, would be arrogant, self-absorbed and ultimately dismissive.

Seemed I would now get the opportunity to tell him so to his face.

I was driven to one of Mumbai's fanciest sports clubs and there escorted to a table on a long terraced verandah. Tea and slices of fruit cake had been laid out, which a waiter in a white buttoned tunic served while I waited.

My host was late, confirming my worst fears. I would give him a piece of my mind, denounce him for the ill-mannered boor he was and leave in a whirl of that self-righteous superiority we elderly Parsis do so well. Nothing he did or said would change my mind!

How wrong I was.

He bounced in just as I was about to start on my second slice of fruit cake with a huge smile, an outstretched arm and a stream of apologies. He held my elbow as we shook hands, a gesture that I found hospitable and respectful.

He sat down and started to talk in a manner so warm and familiar, you might have thought we were two old friends on a regular weekly catch-up.

Good people lack guile.

Instinct told me he was better than that.

He was genuine.

He spoke about himself with candour, a degree of self-deprecation and lively exuberance. Nothing sounded calculated.

Above all, I was struck by the optimism with which he viewed things.

Eternally positive people are an eternal nuisance.

One feels they refuse to see reality.

But his positivity was sincere and more. It was infectious.

The weather was wonderful.

The tea perfect.

The *samosas* delicious.

My jacket beautifully tailored.

Mumbai the greatest city in the world.

He saw the best in everything.

He told me, without any trace of bashfulness, that he had an amazing story to tell, one he thought might encourage others to strive harder and reach higher.

I asked why.

'So many of us Indians believe everything in life is preordained. So we accept and tolerate. I believe that the only thing that is preordained is where you start off in life. Where you end up is entirely in your own hands. I think my story may help some people to realise that.'

I asked why he would choose a retired, old copywriter like myself.

'I am from Gujarat. I am most comfortable speaking in my mother tongue, Gujarati, which you also speak. So I can talk to you in our language, and because you Parsis speak the best English amongst all Indians, you will be able to find the right words to tell my story.'

'Also,' and here the most mischievous smile broke over his face, 'everyone knows Parsis are cowards. So, I know you won't cheat me out of my story or my author's fees.'

I have seldom been so intrigued by an insult.

'But why me?' I persisted. 'There are so many successful Indian authors who write excellent English.'

He leaned towards me as if to let me in on a huge secret.

'Yes, I have been told so, but from what I have seen, all their books are very fat. I think if you use lots of big words, in the end, people will remember the words, not the story.

So, I want someone who will use only a few words.

That way I think my story will be the hero, not some clever language. In advertising, where you come from, it seems you have to tell stories with as few words as possible. That's what I am looking for. Simple. Straightforward.'

After such flattery, I could not bring myself to walk away.

I agreed to hear him out.

'Thank you,' he said graciously, 'but first I have to make one request. I need to do this quickly. Oh, you can take time writing it, but you see, I may not have much time left, so I need to do my part as soon as possible.'

I waited for him to explain himself, but nothing more was forthcoming. In the end, I decided his health and well-being were none of my concern. If he just wanted to talk, what the hell, I would listen.

So, over the next two weeks, we met daily at the same venue.

He spoke while I listened, recorded and devoured slices of that excellent fruit cake.

He spoke candidly, spontaneously and with an innocence I found quite disarming.

He never tried to make himself a hero.

He never blamed others for bad decisions he had made.

His words were simple, his narrative straightforward.

He spoke from the heart, and the tale he had to tell, despite my best efforts to listen as dispassionately as possible, went straight to mine.

After a few sessions, one thing became very apparent to me. I could not tell his story. No writer could.

What he had to say was so personal, so much a part of the man himself, only he could, should, tell it.

So I decided that I would put things down exactly as he spoke them, in the first person, in his narrative style, his words, his sequence of events, his homespun wisdom. As far as possible, I would keep his expressions, his descriptive flair and above all, his humour. All I would do was try and find the right words (as few of them as possible) with which to turn his Gujarati rhythms and idioms into English.

Therefore, the translation you are about to read is mine. But the voice is entirely his.

Shapoor Batliwalla

1

FLASHBACK TO THE BEGINNING

Mumbai. The 2000's

I have to confess that I bought my rickshaw driver's license even before I had sat at the controls of a rickshaw. Two thousand rupees, a few quick touches of the forelock to flatter the clerical classes, and I was the licensed driver of a vehicle I had never ever ridden in.

Ah, the glory of India. Land of 'robbertunity'.

The day I arrived in Mumbai from my tiny village in Gujarat, I realised that rickshaw driving was the sort of job I had been hoping to find.

My fellow villager Hariharan, who had moved to Mumbai some eight months earlier, picked me up from Chhatrapati

Shivaji Terminus in his bright-blue, three-wheel Tempo van and drove me north towards his home, a tiny cabin he shared with five others.

I stared at the magnificence of the city, wide eyed in disbelief at the height of the buildings, the snarl of the traffic, the hordes of people on the streets. It was a sensory sucker punch!

Until this day, I had only ever known the sights and sounds of my sleepy little village, some two hours east of Ahmedabad.

In our village, life was unhurried and gently paced. The silence of the day, disturbed only by the occasional bellow of a buffalo pulling a plough or the squabbles of children young enough to be allowed to play rather than help tend the fields.

Village life is slow motion. Mumbai seemed to be permanently on fast-forward. Most surprising though, was the activity taking place around us. The two roads that ran through our village were just that, roads, traversed occasionally by tractor or bullock cart.

But in Mumbai, the roads were far more than just channels of transport. They were, depending on the area we drove through, a marketplace, a centre of commerce, a cricket pitch, a meeting hall and, in some cases, home to those who seemed perfectly happy to reside there. I saw people cooking and eating, buying and selling, sitting and sleeping laughing and living on the roadsides or, in some cases, on the roads themselves.

How friendly and convivial, I thought.

In those first few minutes, I knew in my heart that I was going to love this city.

The confusion, the chaos, the camaraderie.

The colours. The smells. The noise.

I did not think things could get more exciting until we crossed north over a stretch of road Hariharan called Mahim Causeway, and I caught my first sight of those magnificent little three-wheeled machines, buzzing about like busy black-and-yellow flies.

They seemed to flitter through the traffic unfettered by rule or regulation, weaving and ducking past larger, dangerous-looking vehicles with absolute careless abandon.

The Mumbai rickshaw! I was mesmerised.

I gazed enviously at the men seated at the driver's seat, no doors to box them in, their khaki shirts blowing free in the breeze. Behind the drivers I saw proof of just how versatile these little mechanical marvels were. Although they carried only a small bench seat for two, perhaps three, passengers, the limited space in no way curbed the uses to which they were put.

I saw a mother with four children in school uniform, all huddled together, one child, pen in hand, apparently finishing his homework.

I saw tradesmen with hods of bricks, or boxes of tiles or planks of wood, crammed into the back, holding onto their cargo for fear it would shoot out the sides around a sharp corner.

I saw dhobis with bundles of clothes, tiffin carriers with long trays of lunch boxes, and even a man and his three dogs, all on the one tiny seat, enjoying the wind as it rushed through the little doorless cabin. Little three-wheeled beetles, more tall than wide, that transformed themselves with each passenger's need from school bus to delivery van to ambulance.

I knew instinctively that I had found my calling.

My poor father, bound to the rhythms of the land and the seasons, not to mention the demands of his creditors, was forced to work his tiny farm from daybreak to sunset.

'The ideal job,' he would tell us, as my mother massaged his aching back, 'would be one where you can choose how much you want to do. Go to work, or lie on you charpoy all day. It's up to you.'

I quickly realised a rickshaw would be exactly that. I would only work the hours I wanted to, dictated by the demands of my stomach and, more importantly, the hungers of my imagination. That is, how many movies I wanted to watch in a week.

Deepika Padukone, actress extraordinaire and the most beautiful woman in the world, would control my earning power.

I vowed that when she was on the screen, I would be off the streets and in a seat in front of her.

Yes, I am a Bollywood believer. A film fanatic. A junk junkie. Always have been.

Our village square housed our one communal village TV, and my earliest memories are of me, cross-legged on the ground, staring at the screen, captivated by everything I saw and heard. A fantasy world that gave us a glimpse of life unlike anything our little village could ever offer.

Here, men were tall and well built, with deep voices and deeper pockets. They never seemed to have to collect cow dung for fuel or beg their banks for loans or struggle to make ends meet.

The women were always perfectly dressed, wore expensive jewellery and were always so fair skinned. You knew they couldn't cook or till a field or milk a goat, but who cared? They danced like angels and sang in beautiful, childlike voices, a sure sign that they were as pure and unspoiled as a fresh tin of ghee.

I watched it all.

The romances, the comedies, the dramas, the action thrillers.

I took them in as soil absorbs rain.

I never questioned the premise that life always has a happy ending or that a man always ends up with the girl he loves.

I believed absolutely that we Indians always outsmarted our enemies or that the mega-rich, uncaring and ungenerous at first, would experience some cathartic, life-changing event that would transform them into kind, charitable repentants.

Who was I to question the probability of what Bollywood showed me? If it happened in the movies, surely it must also happen in life!

I clung to that belief as tightly as I could.

After all, I had never heard of anyone from our village, with limited skills and an even more limited education, going to a large city, making a fortune and coming back as a kindly, compassionate landowner who devoted himself to the welfare of his fellow villagers.

But I had seen it in the movies.

Rags to riches, serf to sahib, pauper to prince was not an uncommon Bollywood theme and for those of us who started life with nothing, it was a dream we clung to.

In fact, it was the pursuit of that dream that drove me and millions more like me to our big cities.

There, Bollywood told me, is where my transformation from woebegone to wealthy would take place.

So, I moved to Mumbai, got my rickshaw license and waited for fate to come along and turn me from nobody to somebody.

Of course, until she did, I had to earn my keep, which meant I had to find a rickshaw to drive.

The beauty of arriving into a large city from a tiny Indian village is that others from your village who have preceded you are beholden by a sort of communal bond to help out. So, through a friend of a friend of a friend, a vast word of mouth network India perfected long before the advent of social media, I was introduced to Sri Ram Lal Gopilal, owner of four rickshaws all bearing names of goddesses he hoped would help deliver him from the cycle of rebirth.

Before I proceed any further, I have to state here that every single name used in this account is entirely fictitious, be it names of people, localities, businesses, bars or clubs.

Yes, it all happened in Mumbai. Every other name is an invention.

Much of what I am about to tell you still exists and still happens.

Many of these people are still out there striving to make a living, to make ends meet.

I would never want to jeopardise their livelihoods or lives by divulging information that could help the forces of retribution identify them. And I certainly do not want to jeopardise mine.

Anyway, Ram Lal (as we shall call him), owner, operator, ogre, agreed to let me have his oldest rickshaw at 30% over the rate most rickshaw drivers rented their three-wheelers.

Her name was painted boldly across her rear.

She was Saraswati. Goddess of art, music, learning and wisdom.

This 30% surcharge compensated for my complete inability to drive any sort of motorised vehicle.

'You have a license, so legally you can drive. Any damage you cause, you pay for,' he said, handing me the papers I would need to show if ever I were stopped by the police.

Fortunately, in India, ignorance is no barrier to achievement, and once again, village bonds came to my assistance.

Hariharan (remember, not his real name), who drove his three-wheeled van delivering gas canisters around Mumbai, gave me a quick lesson in gear changing, braking and accelerating, blowing the horn (unnecessary really, as this is a talent all Indians are born with) and fiddling the meter (ditto).

There were no lessons on road rules, traffic regulations or safety procedures for the simple reason that no rickshaw driver in the entire Mumbai metropolitan area has any knowledge, or need, of these sorts of things.

After a few practice circuits around Mount Mary, past Mehboob Studios, and up and down K Road (still have not mastered the hill start) with Hariharan hanging out the side of the rickshaw shouting instructions at me, Saraswati and I were on our way.

We were open for business.

Some think that the life of a Mumbai rickshaw driver must be hell on earth, given the traffic, the heat and the obduracy of our B.E.S.T. bus drivers.

But I was in heaven.

All day I had the wind in my hair and the rich aromas of a fragrant land in my nostrils.

From the smell of the frying *jalebi* at Pali Naka, to the rich biryani aromas behind St Stanislaus school, to the sweet scent of the *chaat*[1] opposite Elco arcade, every road in Bandra had its own rewards.

I practised with joy the art of hitting safety humps and pot-holes at just the right speed and angle needed to cause passengers to fly off their seat and hit their heads on the crossbar above it.

Entertainment at every corner.

And every day I relished the challenge of beating buses, chauffeured limousines and the sworn enemy of all rickshaw drivers, the black-and-yellow taxis of Mumbai, to the same small stretch of road.

Most people have to pay to experience real excitement.

I got paid for living it.

The other great advantage of driving a rickshaw, as I found out in no time at all, was that my little machine was more than just my workspace.

It also doubled as my home.

Curling up on the back seat, I saved on the rent I would have had to pay to hire a tiny corner of some dingy tenement

---

1 The name derives from the Hindi word *chatna* or 'to lick your fingers.' A term for Indian street snacks used long before some Southern Colonel started flogging fried chicken.

in some sprawling slum. I suspect that's why nature has made most of us Indians small.

In life, you pay for the amount of space you take up.

Little bodies, lower rents.

Or, given my ability to curl up on the back seat of my rickshaw, no rent at all.

But what about the other facilities a human needs? you will ask.

How can a mobile home provide that?

Well, in villages all over India, when nature calls we answer by walking down to the fields, finding a secluded spot and settling down to appreciate the beauty around us.

The warmth of the sun, the scent of freshly tilled earth, the contrast of green fields against a clear blue sky.

We learn to take in the wonders of nature while simultaneously we relieve ourselves of the same.

How multifaceted we Indians are!

What was good for me in the village was good for me in the city.

The rocks off Carter Road made for a peaceful, even contemplative, toilet space.

At the other end of Bandra, the clear pools off Land's End made for a bathing area with a never-ending supply of water.

I am ashamed to admit that some of my misguided countrymen chose to wash and relieve themselves on the same stretch of coast.

But not me.

The demarcation between squatting and scrubbing has always been very important to me.

No doubt any non-Indians reading this will wrinkle their noses.

'Dirty fellow, doing his private business in the open.'

But think of this.

In your fully enclosed Western-style bathroom, you bathe in the same room in which you have just relieved yourself, usually all within a few feet, with no breeze to waft away the evidence of your labours, no sun to turn it into harmless dust. I, on the other hand, put five kilometres of fresh air and clean ocean between the areas I defecate and wash in.

No harmful sprays to dispel odours.

No trees felled to wipe my bottom.

No precious drinking water wasted.

No chemicals used to clean my toilet.

Now which do you think is the healthier option?

Our way has always been to let nature clear away what nature produces. When man tries to improve on it, it seems to me, he just makes a bigger mess.

I know your next response.

'Bah...what does a simple *rickshawalla* know about bathrooms or health or the environment?'

Well, in a way, that is what this story is about.

The story of how destiny and a little bit of foolhardiness can take a man all the way from the rocks off Carter Road to a life of comfort.

In those early days I honestly believed that my life could not get any better and I wanted no more than the simple pleasures that Saraswati, and the total freedom she brought me, offered. A masala chai morning and afternoon, two simple meals a day, a *bidi* or two and of course, the movie tickets that were my gateway to a world of luxury and avarice I could only dream about.

I suppose if anyone has to take the blame for where I am today, it would have to be Bollywood.

Everything in a typical Bollywood world reeks of money.

Luxury apartments, multi-storey bungalows, holidays to exotic locations and, of course, bejewelled women you knew would cost a fortune to keep, dress or romance.

(Even Deepika, goddess though she is, would probably expect more than a glucose biscuit and *kadak chai*[2] if one were lucky enough to take her out).

Bollywood whets the appetite for the very things one cannot have.

I suppose that's what dreams are about. What Indian movies are all about.

The unwashed salivating over the unattainable.

Still, it's all simple aspirational stuff you may think, no harm done.

Wrong.

For impressionable young people, Bollywood is mighty dangerous.

You see, the best of the good life it portrays, the whisky drinking, dance-girl fondling, money-burning pleasures it

---

2 An Indian institution; tarted up tea.

offers are enjoyed almost exclusively by the villains in the story, the 'bad guys'.

The hero is usually some simpering wimp who lives with his mother, goes to the temple twice a day and has a shitty menial job in some shitty office or government department.

Menial we all have.

Money is what we don't.

The drug dealers, the greedy politicians, the smugglers, evil landowners and gang leaders, they were the ones who had the best of everything.

They had the girlfriends with the largest breasts.

They had the fanciest clothes, the thickest gold chains and devoured entire flocks of tandoori chickens in one sitting.

You see, my friends, this is the simple, insidious truth about Bollywood. It turns bastardry into a highly desirable lifestyle.

Of course, in their make-believe world, you know that in the end, the hero will win, and the bad guy will be vanquished.

But after a few months in a big, unrelenting city like Mumbai, you soon realise that good is merely a cinematic device, created solely to appease the Government Board of Film Censors.

In real life, when does good really ever make an appearance?

Does good ever find a poor man a much-needed kidney?

Does good ever turn the dust in a beggar's bowl into *dahl*?

Does good ever pay off the traffic policeman who wants a bribe and suspends your license until you are forced to steal the money you need to be able to go back to earning an honest living?

No my friends, this is India.

Good, much like our Parliament, seems to be on recess most of the year.

So, while the bad guy may fall to his knees and beg forgiveness in the cinema, in real life he is visibly prosperous, driving large foreign cars, seated in the VIP section of IPL matches and throwing mega parties in Dubai.

In the cinema, the bad guy lives to provide retribution.

In real life, he just lives happily ever after.

As I talk about this, I wonder, am I just making excuses? Perhaps.

But believe me, when you have nothing, getting what you want becomes far more important than how you get it.

Hunger gives one's mouth absolute priority over one's morals.

That's why, when Chotu Avzal, aka Avzal Bhai, shot Rakesh Dehliwalla in the back of my rickshaw, I did more than just turn a blind eye.

I took a hold of my destiny, got my washcloth out of its storage compartment and helped him clean off the bloodstains splattered over Saraswati's red plastic passenger seat.

2

EXPAND THE PLOT

I was almost done for the night.

Saraswati and I were parked at the very end of Land's End in Bandra West, near the entrance to the old Portuguese fort, watching the evening crowd making merry on the foreshore and waiting for a suitable fare.

Do you know Bandra?

It is a little jewel of a suburb, just north of Mumbai city itself.

I love it not because film stars and famous cricketers live there but because of all of Mumbai's suburbs, Bandra has, to this day, retained some of it's old-world charm.

Yes, there are the usual multi-storey buildings and crowded streets of modern India, but if you know where to look, you will still find narrow tree-lined by-lanes with tiny bungalows dating back to the early 1900s.

Yes, it is shrouded in the grey concrete of progress that most of Mumbai seems to have had poured over it, but it still has areas that are green, verdant reminders of its past.

Yes, there is all the hustle and hurry of a large city, but turn off the bustling main roads, and you will still find the friendliness and charm of a small village.

Looking out as it does on to the Arabian Sea, it gets the first drops of monsoon rain to break the heat of an incessant summer.

It enjoys cooling breezes when the rest of Mumbai swelters, and the sky over the ocean treats onlookers to light shows of spectacular colours. The rosy pinks of dawn. The burning ambers of sunset. The angry blacks of monsoon clouds.

Sadly today, the most prevalent colour in the skies over Mumbai is a gloomy industrial grey, but if you have to put up with the grey cloud of progress that envelops the city most days, I'd rather put up with it in Bandra than anywhere else.

You will understand its appeal when I tell you that in 1661, the Portuguese, showing uncharacteristic largesse, gave all of Mumbai to Charles I as a dowry on his marriage to Catherine of Portugal (doesn't say much for poor Catherine, does it?).

All of Mumbai that is, except the village of Bandra. That they kept for themselves.

Of course, since laying claim to Mumbai in around 1535, the Portuguese did some of their best work in Bandra. In 1560, one priest alone, father Manuel Gomes converted 2000 villagers to Christianity, displaying a level of zeal and industry the indolent locals must have found truly dazzling, if not downright divine.

Every day, when I ride past St Andrew's Church on Hill Road, I marvel at the fact that it was built almost 50 years before the Taj Mahal.

But while the Taj today is merely a tourist attraction in disrepair, St Andrew's is a vibrant, functioning beacon of faith for Bandra's many Christians.

To this day, babies are baptised, marriages are solemnised, masses are held and absolution is given in this glorious building, which may have none of the fame of the Taj but has far more relevance.

I suppose that summarises a key difference in the architectural legacy of these two great religions that came to India.

Islam built and battered.

Christianity constructed and converted.

For these reasons and more, I am an adopted Bandra-ite. It is my home, and I love it.

So, there I was, sitting at Land's End and waiting to see what the evening would bring me or, more correctly, where it would take me.

Unfortunately, everyone who approached me that night seemed to live in distant suburbs like Malad or Thane or Versova.

Normally, I would have leapt at the opportunity to score a large fare, but I had a ticket for the 11.30 p.m. showing of *A Fool for Love* at the Lustrous Diamond triplex cinema in Bandra, and as with most Indians, I would rather give up a kidney than forego a cinema ticket.

Word was it featured some stunning dance numbers, shot to show off the finest attributes of Miss Pinky Pal Kumari, third runner-up in the recent Miss India contest and our latest 'bombshell' discovery.

Equally inviting, playing opposite her as her love interest and presumably the fool mentioned in the title, was one of our finest, most loved heroes, Bunty Bhaskar.

Although now approaching his mid-fifties, Bunty could still dance, dash about and dish it out with the best of them.

He may visibly be pulling in his middle-aged paunch, but so what? He was still pulling in the crowds.

I am told that in the West, audiences expect romancing couples to be of a similar age. We have no such hang-ups in India.

When it comes to a suitable man, wealth smoothes out even the deepest wrinkles. In our country, marriage is not about the man a woman wants. It's about the man her parents want.

That's why we younger fellows do not expect to be married off in the near future. Who wants to pay for a penniless youth when your dowry can buy you someone who is already comfortably off?

It's the only way parents can make sure that one day, hopefully, their daughter will have the means to look after them.

Anyway, that evening, around 10 p.m., as night fell upon the Bandstand, it appeared my working day was at an end.

Reading this, some of you may conjure up an image of a dark, empty night along a lonely seashore with an eerie silence echoing through deserted streets.

If so, you have never been to an Indian city.

To us, daytime is for making a living.

And night-time is for making a commotion.

You see, in our country it is considered downright un-neighbourly to keep one's opinions, one's music, or one's domestic disputes, to oneself.

So, when India comes home from work, the volume of life is turned up dramatically.

Loud conversations, loud televisions, loud arguments, loud street games, loud dogs chasing loud cats, loud mothers-in-law, loud street vendors, loud horns.

That is our music of the night.

I have heard that foreigners who come here find it irritating and intrusive.

We find it comforting.

To us, it is a reminder that miserable and frightening as life may be, one is never alone on this journey.

Chaos is the soundtrack of our nation and one we enjoy sharing with all around us.

For example, that evening, as I sucked on my *bidi*, sitting back in the driver's seat with my feet up on Saraswati's handlebar, I could hear at least three different Bollywood songs from three different transistors, the gas flames under the teapot at the *chaiwalla*'s stall, the crackle of corn roasting over an open fire, the farts of the man roasting the corn, the bells around the neck of a cow tethered to a nearby tree and the voices of old friends as they took their nightly constitutionals along the promenade.

Which is why at first I almost did not hear the dark, rumbling voice that came to me over my shoulder.

'Bandra East. Take the highway, and I will guide you from there.'

I felt Saraswati list to one side as a heavy body stepped aboard and then settled onto the passenger seat.

Rude bastard, I thought, getting in without so much as a hello or, more importantly, that crucial moment of eye contact that allows a *rickshawalla* the opportunity to judge whether the passenger looks like he has the means to pay for his fare or is likely do a runner at the Bandra Circle traffic lights.

I turned to tell him that that he should look for another ride as my evening belonged to Miss Pinky Pal Kumari and her bouncing blouse, but as I turned to give him the brush-off, the words froze in my throat like drops of milk turning into *kulfi*.

I saw behind me a crop of thick curly hair atop two eyes that burned as fiercely as the headlights on a Bandra locomotive. I saw a dark, pitted complexion; skin ravaged over time by acne and recycled razor blades.

I saw a flat, widespread nose, testimony to a million battles lost. I saw a thin scar that started just under the right cheekbone and ran down to his upper lip.

And under it, most terrifyingly, I saw the thickest, shiniest gold chain that money could buy.

I knew who it was.

I knew I had to be very careful with what I said next.

And instinctively I also knew that the next few moments would probably determine the future course of my life.

3

PRESENT THE BACKSTORY

At this point, for anyone reading this who is not a Mumbaikar, I need to digress a bit to explain to you the geography of greed as it exists in Mumbai today.

Centuries ago, Mumbai was an archipelago of seven islands.

The British, who eventually took it over from the Portuguese, found that all too messy and fragmented for their liking, so over the course of 150 years, through several landfill projects, they turned it into one large land mass.

By this time in our history, their policy of divide and conquer had long given way to their even more expedient policy of extort and export, and it was much more efficient to loot from one central location than several dispersed ones.

Along the way, they also changed its original name of Mumba, in honour of the goddess Mumbadevi, to Bombay.

If you look at a map of India closely, Mumbai today is that elongated scrotum that projects out of the mainland of India, just below the protruding belly that is Gujarat.

The seven islands are now firmly attached to each other and to the body of India by an umbilical cord of bridges, roads and tenements, all built on reclaimed land.

The names of those seven islands are now the names of the seven districts of South Mumbai: the Isle of Mumbai, Colaba, Little Colaba (or Old Woman's Island, as it was known), Mahim, Mazagaon, Parel and Worli are now one big amalgamated land mass that has expanded to include areas such as Andheri, Juhu, Kandivali, Borivili to the north and Thane and Mulund towards the east.

Along its west coast, as mentioned earlier, sits the Arabian Sea, and towards the east, past the deep, boggy marshlands that line the rivers and creeks that once separated Mumbai from the mainland, the land stretches out towards the Deccan Plateau and the rest of India.

Over the years, as this city grew and prospered, there emerged several enterprising businessmen who sought new and interesting ways to take advantage of her newfound prosperity.

Now you may think that I am talking of what the newspapers so wrongly call 'gangs'.

Not at all.

A gang is simply a group of unruly young men, stealing and looting indiscriminately, bullying and beating up the defenceless.

We already had the British for that.

They had long mastered the gangster-like art of stealing from the poor (us) to feed the rich (themselves), leaving no fat for others to pick off.

No, I am talking about organisations that actually had to create new areas of business. They found opportunities where none had existed before and developed these into profitable long-term enterprises with well-defined sales goals, expansion plans and annual growth targets.

Most lucrative of these were the businesses that controlled the coastal regions where the dhows from the Middle East could land their contraband cargo.

Gold has always been a major source of profit, bought cheap in the souks of the Middle East and jacked up in price to feed the insatiable Indian hunger for ostentation.

Indeed, the modernisation of India is best traced by the items smuggled in over the years.

Gold (timeless) and, over the years, alcohol, diesel oil, Parker pens, Levi jeans, electronics, watches, cameras, digital phones and, eventually, computers.

Today, smuggling has reached new levels of sophistication with large caches of osmium dust, used to add power to nuclear weapons, making their way from Russia to Kazakhstan to Iraq and from there the time-honoured journey to Mumbai.

Sad isn't it that we have gone from wanting things that enhanced our lives to that which could well end it?

The same boats, filled now with Indian bhang, *charas*, and agarwood (the 'wood of the gods' used to make oudh, the perfume that pervades the armpit of all Arabia) then ply their way westwards, making the route between Mumbai and the Arabian peninsula one of the oldest, busiest and most profitable trade routes in the world.

But while smuggling might represent the romantic, even exotic end of their business activities, these businesses also diversified into the more mundane, domestic areas of profit.

Isn't it interesting that over the course of evolution man first used his brain to come up with useful things like language, mathematics and the automatic *chapatti* maker?

Then, having tired himself through all that strenuous intellectual activity, he came up with his much-needed modes of relaxation: gambling, prostitution, drugs, bootlegging and money lending.

Today, governments control and profit from the former areas.

And the private enterprise I am talking about, from the latter.

At one time in our history, every district had its own organisation trying to make the most of the opportunities presented to it by the very human need for pleasure.

They squabbled and fought with each other to expand their territories and establish a pecking order. Eventually, through the well-known business practice of acquisition and annihilation, the smaller businesses became parts of a larger whole.

Today, all this private enterprise, in all of the land mass of Mumbai from Vasal Creek in the north down to the very southern tip of Colaba are run by two large, powerful organisations that are as well managed and staffed as any large business in India.

All the North, from Gorai down to about Kalina, are under the control of an overlord I will, for the sake of my future well-being, call Narendra Salgaonkar. From the Bandra Kurla Complex down to the tip of Navy Nagar, you find the fiefdom of the equally fictitiously named big boss Bade Mian.

Both organisations employ a similar corporate structure. Under these two CEOs, sit their seconds-in-command, or MDs, if you will. They are tasked with the responsibility of keeping an eye on day-to-day business while the CEO concentrates more on diversification and sales expansion.

Next come a series of area managers controlling a district of about 15 square miles each. They report directly to the MD, who is solely in charge of meting out reward or punishment based on profit figures achieved.

Within his territory, the area managers appoint their own sales directors who look after various streams of the business.

So, in corporate terms, there would be a Director of Drugs, Director of Brothels and Dance Halls, Director of Liquor (local and imported), Director of Unpaid Debts, Director of Lending and Collecting and so on.

And finally, working for these directors would be a series of footmen, each with their own skills and proclivities.

Strong-arm specialists, stand-over men, pimps, extortionists, money lenders, gambling den managers, collection agents and so on.

Wherever there was money to be made, you'd find an organisation man charged with the responsibility to make as much of it as possible, whatever the means and at whatever the cost (to others).

Needless to say, relations between the two organisations were tense at the best of times, erupting occasionally into selective warfare.

A body found floating in Bassein Creek would be quickly followed by a decapitated head being discovered along the railway lines at Matunga.

A burning dance hall in Mahim would mean that tomorrow a similar fate would befall a drinking den in Borivili.

An unwritten rule of retribution allowed these organisations to keep each other in check.

Being pragmatic business people, however, they kept out of each other's way as much as possible; the Mumbai police happily kept out of everyone's way, and so a tenuous peace prevailed over Mumbai.

This brings me back to the burning eyes and scarred skin staring at me from my back seat.

Chottu Avzal, or Avzal Bhai, as his colleagues called him, was known to all of us little people who frequented the occasional gambling den or drinking parlour (the dance halls and bespoke brothels being well beyond our means).

He was a man to be avoided at the best of times or, should fate insist on a face-to-face meeting, be treated with utmost respect.

You see, Avzal Bhai was known in his organisation as 'Manager of Final Solutions'.

Not a man to be refused.

So, with no safe option left to me, I pulled Saraswati's starter lever and awaited his instructions.

Sadly, Miss Pinky Pal Kumari would dance alone tonight.

4

ESTABLISH THE CONFLICT

From Bandstand, down Hill Road, right past the Masjid and then left onto the highway, I drove as if I had suddenly been elected President of the All India Society for Passenger Comfort and Consideration.

Around potholes, within the one lane, slow over speed breakers and with only the occasional bleat of my horn.

Miraculously my driving philosophy had changed from 'the passenger is baggage' to 'the passenger is king'.

Pissing off Avzal Bhai would not be a life-enhancing move.

From the highway, through a series of grunts and jabs to the back of my shoulders, Avzal Bhai guided me around the back of Dharavi, the world's largest, best-serviced and most profitable slum, down to where the road leads to the Maharashtra Nature Park.

There we headed east, turning off the main road just before Naik Nagar. The bitumen gradually turned into a dirt track, getting soggier and more rutted as we neared the furthest reaches of the Mithi River.

Mithi River sounds grand, doesn't it?

In truth it is a rank, stagnant finger of water lined with marshy banks that gave off a stench so vile even Dharavi, the world's least-selective suburb, had stopped well short of encroaching upon it.

By this time, we had left human habitation well behind.

We were in prime mosquito land, each insect so laden with malaria and dengue fever that not even India's spreading population had dared spread this way.

Saraswati slithered and slid along the marshy ground under us until, in the light of her headlamp, we saw a motorcycle parked by the river and a man leaning up against it.

For a moment, I thought I was seeing things. I wanted to jump out of Saraswati and run for my life.

But as I thought about it, I realised that I could well be on the verge of watching history take place.

Fate, I thought, must have a reason for choosing me to be an observer of a seminal moment in determining the future of Mumbai.

For, standing there in the darkness, cigarette in hand and dark glasses on forehead was Rakesh Dehliwalla himself. So called because he was born and bred in Dehli and had brought with him a degree of Northern savagery that greatly disturbed us more cultured Western Indians.

At this juncture I need to digress into something you may think to be irrelevant to this story.

I need to explain why the India–Pakistan problem will never be sorted out: Avzal Bhai was a loyal employee of the organisation headed up by Bade Mian. Rakesh Dehliwalla was District Director of Dadar area for the Narendra clan.

You will have spotted the conflict point.

The Bade Mian organisation, as the name suggests, is predominantly run and staffed by Muslims, Bade Mian being a very Muslim form of address for big man or elder brother.

The Salgaonkar lot is predominantly Hindu.

Human resource experts may frown upon their hiring techniques, but both organisations were staffed almost entirely on the basis of their faith.

The Muslims only trusted each other and saw the Hindus as cowardly bullies who were an eternal obstacle to their aims of expansion and diversification.

The Hindus only trusted each other and saw the Muslims as lower-class interlopers with no real reason for existing.

Religion formed a permanent and insurmountable bond of hatred between the two.

No gunfire was exchanged as long as each kept to its own territory; the Muslims to the south and the Hindus to the north.

From there, behind the safety of their own lines, they could bare their teeth, make threats against each other and generally inflate their egos without anyone really getting hurt.

The problem lay with the middle ground, the disputed districts between their two territories where no clear boundary existed.

Unfortunately, my Mumbai, the areas where I lived and worked, Bandra, Khar and Santa Cruz, lay exactly in that disputed middle ground.

It was land where no official border existed, other than in the minds of the two CEOs.

Both claimed it. Both fought for it. Both would happily spill blood (the other persons of course) over it.

Now obviously there is a simple solution to all this.

Meet somewhere over a nice hot butter chicken, pull out a map of Mumbai, draw out a clear line between the two territories and abide by it.

A little give and take.

A bit of back and forth.

A little common sense and all conflict comes to an end.

But it will never happen.

Unfortunately, for the parties involved, agreeing on a border is not about the size of the prize to be had.

It's about the size of cock to be lost.

For either to cede an inch of land (despite the foot they may be getting in return), would be a source of deep humiliation, seen as downright cowardice in the eyes of their supporters.

Not worthy of respect and possibly triggering a change of leadership.

Sadly, in the war of egos, compromise equals capitulation.

So, year after year, they arm themselves with newer, bigger weapons and celebrate the ensuing conflict as proof of their manhood.

That's why there will never be a solution.

The problem has become the prize.

So you see, if Rakesh Dehliwalla, a District Director of the Salgaonkar organisation, was involved in a clandestine meeting with Avzal Bhai, a manager of the Bade Mian organisation, I was probably going to be a witness (involuntarily of course) to something big.

As we got closer to the motorcycle, my passenger barked at me again.

'Stop here, boy.'

I turned off the engine.

Saraswati burped, gurgled and went silent. Simultaneously, her tiny headlamp went out, and we were enveloped in a deep, and for me deeply disturbing, darkness.

'Go take a walk. Stay close, but make sure you keep your ears closed.'

Quickly I hopped out and walked along the edge of the creek, at first keeping my back to the rickshaw and whatever may be about to transpire on her back seat.

As I got further away however, I was overtaken by a fundamental human weakness. The one where we find curiosity a more compelling force than caution.

From the shadows, I could not but help myself from looking over my shoulder at the rickshaw and the two men there.

I saw Rakesh Dehliwalla walk from his motorcycle to the rickshaw and look in.

For several minutes he stood there talking to Avzal Bhai, who was still seated within.

Suddenly and without warning, Avzal Bhai's arm shot out, grabbed the other by his throat and dragged him into the rickshaw.

Saraswati then began to rock ominously.

I must admit, friends, my mind started to wander into disturbing areas.

Was I watching a mere struggle or something altogether more fruity and forbidden?

Was my story heading for the box-office death of an R rating?

The answer came in a flash. The flash of light that accompanies a gunshot.

The sound of it roared over the empty marshes, cut through the faint sounds of humanity emanating from the distant slums and rolled away, rumbling and echoing into the distance.

For what seemed like an eternity nothing moved; no one spoke, and I stood there, as frozen to the spot as an ice *gola* sticks to the tongue.

Then gradually, the frogs rediscovered their voices, the crickets resumed their humming and time, moving forward again, began to run out for me.

5

PRESENT THE DILEMMA

'I know you are there, frog. Come here.' To me, Avzal Bhai's
voice sounded like a summons to the gallows.

Pivotal moment this.

If the movie of my life ever gets made, this is where the
camera will close in on the actor's face, his eyes narrowing and
brow furrowing as if deep in thought, weighing his options
(Bunty Bhaskar does really good contemplation).

Will he obey or will he run? Fight or fly? Get killed or get
away?

A lifetime's worth of options and their outcomes flashed
through my mind in seconds.

I had witnessed what Avzal Bhai's employers would probably call a Permanent Cessation of Ongoing Discussions.

If I ran, I would instantly become a threat to Avzal Bhai's
peace of mind.

I'd be hiding in sewers and eating rats.

Not a good way to spend the few days you may have left to you.

If I walked up to him, begging for mercy on trembling knees, I would probably get shot in the face.

Either way, fate seemed hell-bent on bringing an end to my life.

Ah well, I am after all a Gujarati.

If I am about to die, I may as well see if I can derive some profit from it.

Trying to muster up as much swagger as I could, I walked up to Saraswati and looked inside.

Avzal Bhai sat there as before, looking as unflustered and undisturbed as he had been on the ride down. No change other than the ugly-looking pistol resting in his hands. It had a steel-blue muzzle and wood-grained insets on the handle.

Next to him, Rakesh Dehliwalla lay sprawled along the seat, arms and legs akimbo, his head resting against my beloved Saraswati's canopy.

I forgave him.

Clearly he could not have held it up on his own given the two rupee coin sized hole in his temple.

I saw a spattering of matter and blood on the seat and Avzal Bhai's face and shoulders.

Luckily, Rakesh being a Northerner had a skull thick enough to stop the bullet from exiting his head completely and ruining the plastic sheeting that made up Saraswati's canopy.

To my relief, she was dirty but undamaged.

Avzal Bhai's eyes never left me as he let me look over the scene.

I noticed that the gun, which had lain flat in his palm, was now upright and pointing at my chest.

'What do you think has just happened, boy?'

This was it. The moment between life and death.

Deference, tears, pleading ignorance, none of that was going to work.

Every decent Bollywood scriptwriter will tell you that when you arrive at a dramatic crossroad, the difference between an extended run or box-office death, is not in the decision you make but in the dialogue you deliver.

'Yes sir,' I started off. 'A slimy snake that needed stamping out has finally met the end it deserves.'

I saw the twitch of surprise in Avzal Bhai's eyes.

'You know who this is?' he asked.

'Avzal Bhai, every Mumbaikar knows about this Northern scum who has come here and tried to take over that which is rightfully ours. Unlike your organisation, the people he works for are a filthy, untrustworthy mob who hire these out-of-town interlopers to do what we locals could do perfectly well ourselves. No class, Avzal Bhai,' I said, spitting on Rakesh's body for added effect.

(I figured of the two men in the rickshaw, he was the least likely to take umbrage.)

'The sooner strong men like you put an end to them all, the better for us all!'

When one is not brave, one has to turn to bravado.

For a few moments, he said nothing, clearly taken aback. It looked to me as if he was appraising my words and reviewing all options over in his mind.

'Where are you from, boy?'

'Gujarat, sir, just over the border. But Mumbai is my home.'

He looked me up and down.

Then the crunch question.

'Muslim or Hindu?'

This one I was ready for.

'With respect, sir, I am both.

I respect the optimism of Hinduism and the realism of Islam.

I hate both, the class system of the one and the intolerant nature of the other.

I love the sounds of the bells in our temples and the Muezzin's chants from our mosques.

I agree with the Hindu interpretation of fate and the Muslim interpretation of fatalism.

I love Amitabh Bachchan and Aamir Khan.

I understand a Hindu's devotion to many Gods and a Muslim's need for only one.

I can be as forgiving as a Hindu and as faithful as a Muslim.

It's not that I don't believe in any one religion.

It's just that I believe more in the qualities we are born with rather than the ones being sold to us by Brahmins or mullahs or priests.

You see, sir, I am more than a Hindu or a Muslim.

I am an Indian!'

I paused there to see how this drivel was being received.

For a moment nothing. Then slowly he pulled back the hammer of his pistol and pointed it at my chest.

'That is the biggest load of bullshit I have ever heard boy. Babble like that deserves to be silenced forever.'

Despite the menace of him cocking the hammer, I have to tell you, I was more angered than alarmed at his response.

Having sat through eleven screenings of *Brother Brother* (where Sameer Kapoor and Riaz Khan play twins separated at birth and brought up as sworn interfaith enemies until they find love, forgiveness, and their long-lost mother), I knew I had mastered that speech pretty much as written.

Word for word.

When Sameer delivered it to Riaz and the weeping mother, not a dry eye in the house!

On the punchline about being an Indian, on every one of the eleven occasions I heard it, there was a spontaneous outburst of applause, whistling, foot-stamping and *wah wah's*.

What's more, *Brother Brother* ran for 53 weeks near continuously, so I knew the dialogue was not worthy of his scorn.

Which could only mean he was being disparaging of my delivery? How dare he!

'What's your name, boy?'

For the first time in this conversation, I had to pause.

You see, the one thing every cinema-goer knows is that to be a successful and respected villain, you needed a catchy, awe-inspiring, fear-evoking name.

Indian cinema excels at it.

Mogambo. Lion. Dr Dang. Cheddi Singh. Mr Robert. Sukhi Lal.

And of course the greatest, the ever-feared and revered Gabbar Singh.

These were names not to be trifled with.

They are names that conjure up visions of unimaginable bastardry and horror.

My name, on the other hand, is Geetanshu Garjee Bhanchadia.

Now you know why I never sent money home to my parents and have waited so late in my story to reveal it.

My first name, despite all my pleas, gets shortened to Geetu or, worse, Geetie, which among Indian names is so feminine it's downright demeaning.

Unfortunately, my middle name rhymes with *darjee*, or tailor, a lowly trade and often thrown at me as a euphemism for my lowly caste.

And worst of all, my last name, when truncated by those of mischievous intent, becomes *bhanchod*.[3]

If you speak Hindi, you will know that that is the road to a lifetime of derision and despair.

So when Avzal Bhai asked me my name, a perfectly innocent question, I could not bring myself to reveal my shame.

I needed something short, snappy and sexy that men would tremble at and women would disrobe for. But what?

I stood there, one arm on Saraswati's canopy, a foot resting on her running board when suddenly, I knew who I was.

She, my goddess of wisdom, had shared some with me.

Imitating the slow, menacing delivery with which Gabber Singh had chilled a generation of moviegoers and in the

---

3 Too embarrassing to explain. Best if you just Google it.

hushed tones usually reserved for the truly evil, I looked him in the eye and whispered, 'They call me Ricki!'

He cocked his head to one side, staring at me, my fate still undecided.

Then he burst out laughing.

'And I suppose your last name is Shah?'

He slapped his thigh, delighted by his own joke. He thought himself hilarious, the way he had so cleverly parodied my profession.

I groaned in pain.

Should I tell him that I thought 'Ricki Shah' so puerile, so base, so unimaginative a pun it would not even make it into the shooting script of a South Indian film?

Instead, I laughed as it were the cleverest witticism ever.

'Very clever, sir, thank you. From now on, please call me Ricki Shah.'

By introducing the notion of the future, I'd hoped he'd think my cockiness warranted me having one.

As he wiped the tears from his eyes, I noticed that the gun was now again lying flat in his hand, pointing at Saraswati's windscreen rather than my stomach.

Was this crap really going to work? I wondered.

'You, Mr smart-arse Ricki Shah who talks so much…tell me, what should I do with you?'

I seized the moment with both hands.

'Avzal Bhai, you should take me on as your soldier and your servant. I am hard-working, obey orders, have few scruples and will be 100% loyal to you and you alone.

I will watch your back, hate your enemies, keep an eye on your friends and follow you into any situation no matter how dangerous.

I will cook your breakfast, clean your gun, bargain with your pimp, buy your booze or make it at your home if you prefer, and drive you around, day or night.

I will steal for you, break legs for you, collect debts for you and if I have to, kill for you.

And if I ever let you down, I will expect you to kill me.

Now, may I please help you throw this putrefying Punjabi *pakoda* into the marshes and clean his blood off your face and hands?'

No reply came forth.

That's it Ricki (I really liked the first name). You've overplayed your hand. He can see you for the phoney you are, and it all ends now.

Instead, a small, crooked smile stretched over his lips, turning the straight scar on his cheek into the curved bulge of a *bunya*'s belly.

He unlocked the hammer on his pistol, and with the barrel, he pointed to the inert body slumped next to him.

'Put him on his motorcycle,' he ordered.

I started to carry Rakesh Dehliwalla towards the bike.

With every step, my heart beat faster and faster.

Not because the dog from Dehli weighed a ton but because I suspected that finally, my days of shitting on the rocks off Carter Road might be coming to an end.

6

UNVEIL THE UNDERWORLD

I headed back towards Bandra as instructed.

As we drove, I heard Avzal Bhai making several phone calls while I kept replaying the events of the evening in my head, the scene we'd just played out by the river.

'Do you have any rope in this rickshaw?' he'd asked, as I dragged his victim towards his motorcycle.

Every rickshaw driver always has.

Sadly, the pride we feel in Indian engineering in no way bolsters the confidence we have in its reliability.

One never knew when the little two-stroke, 165cc engine of a rickshaw would choose to imitate our urban water supply and simply stop running.

In India, a tow rope is an essential piece of automotive equipment.

Together we lifted Rakesh, who like a good piece of Indian engineering, lay immobile and leaking fluids.

As per Avzal Bhai's instructions, I sat him on the seat of his motorcycle, his chest on the gas tank, his head on the handlebars.

'Now, boy, tie that arsehole on with the rope. Make sure it stays on tight.'

I looped the rope around his body, under the engine and over his back. Round and round until eventually he looked like a serving of *pan* wrapped in string.

'Now, push the bike into the river. There, where the bank slopes down.'

I put the bike in neutral and grabbing the handlebars, started to push towards the dark. I started at a walk, gradually building up speed as we neared the river's edge.

By the time we got to the bank, I was at a full run, the weight of the bike and body now pulling me down the slope until all I had to do was let go at the last moment. The bike shot over the edge of the bank, sailed a good ten feet or so into the air and landed in the river with a resounding splash.

Then, in a flurry of bubbles and gurgles, the royal arsehole and his Royal Enfield sank into the murky ooze of the Mithi River, food for the frogs, snakes and crustaceans living there.

I wondered if they'd develop a taste for North Indian cuisine?

Avzal Bhai and I then got into Saraswati and at his bidding, I drove back to Bandra, towards the Leelavati Hospital. He directed me to a backstreet lined with restaurants that were now dark and shuttered.

There waiting for us under a large pipal tree was a grey jeep, the old Mahindra and Mahindra open-top kind. Behind the wheel sat one of the ugliest men I had ever seen, black as the night, a face to frighten women and children, underlined by a hideous blue-and-pink bandana around his throat. A gold hoop sat on the lobe of one ear, and of course, the ubiquitous gold chain circled his scrawny neck. He must have been about 25 years old, but his face looked as if it had spent a couple of lifetimes in difficult circumstances. He jumped out as Avzal Bhai approached the car, then stopped, clearly surprised to see me tagging along behind his boss.

Avzal pointed at me.

'This is Ricki (thank God he dropped the last name). He could be of use to us.'

Then to me, he said, 'Leave your rickshaw here, boy, and get in.'

The lackey jumped back behind the wheel. Avzal got in the front next to him. I hopped into the back seat.

Avzal Bhai spoke to me over his shoulder.

'This is Imtiaz. He works for me. Be respectful towards him. For the last several Ramadans he has provided the goat meat for his entire *Mohali*. So remember, no one cuts throats like he can.'

This delivered as matter of factly as if he were telling me that Imtiaz was chief cook at the local *khiri kaleji kabab*[4] stand.

The goat-and-throat specialist started the jeep, and off we headed towards the Mahim Causeway.

---

4 Streetside barbecue, cleverly seasoned and spiced to make hitherto inedible animal parts, absolutely irresistible.

You non-Mumbaikars may wonder why we were leaving Saraswati behind, parked under the tree on that deserted side street.

In a nutshell (and in the opinion of all rickshaw drivers) it is all to do with corrupt politics, municipal greed, subjugation of the working man and the power of the black-and-yellow taxi drivers union.

Mumbai forbids its rickshaws from plying their trade beyond Mahim Causeway or the Worli Sea Link.

North of that, we can go where we please.

South of that we get arrested, we get beaten, our licenses are suspended and, even in some cases, our innocent little three-wheelers are burned.

The official explanation is all about containing traffic chaos, air pollution and relieving congestion.

Nonsense!

Given that there are no greater gridlocks in the world than in South Mumbai and no smoggier cities other than Delhi (filthy Northerners), you'd say that the policy was a joke.

In fact, the policy is the problem.

Without our smaller, nimbler rickshaws, the millions of people travelling South Mumbai's roads have to use cars that guzzle more fuel; ancient ill-maintained taxis that burn oil; or the huge, smoke-belching double-decker buses of the Mumbai Municipal Corporation. All larger vehicles that take up more space, clog more streets, burn more diesel and create greater pollution.

A crazy, discriminatory policy, framed not by logic applied but the lakhs paid.

We turned left at Mahim Church, obviously heading south into prime Bade Mian territory.

We drove along Tulsa Pipe road, which at this time of night had been considerably narrowed by my sleeping countrymen taking up all of the curb and most of the inside lane. Bodies on thin coir mats or in their unfurled bedding rolls. Sheets covering them from head to toe, pulled over their faces in the vain hope of keeping out the exhaust fumes that India emanated night and day.

As I cannot work in South Mumbai for reasons mentioned, it's not an area I know well.

I recognized the Lal Baugh flyover and further, the turn-off to Chinchpokli, but most of the landmarks we passed were unknown to me.

We crossed Byculla Bridge and continued south until finally Imtiaz turned off and in the distance I saw the darkened silhouette of what I later learned was the Nawab Ayaz Mosque.

A few more twists and turns and we finally stopped outside an old three-storey building that had probably been built in the 1800s and been left untouched since.

The roof sagged alarmingly, the entire structure listing to one side as if one ageing hip just could not bear the weight that time had laid upon it.

'Where are we?' I asked Imtiaz as we got out of the jeep and walked towards the building.

'Bhendi Bazaar,' he replied. 'That's all you need to know.'

That told me that we were in the heart of the Muslim area of Mumbai, somewhere between Mohammed Ali Road and Khetwadi, not far from Mumbai's largest market.

Years later, I learned that Bhendi Bazaar was the Indianisation of the phrase 'behind the bazaar', the term the British used to describe the area behind Crawford market. All I knew then was that I, a Hindu, was about to be led into a Muslim stronghold, by a Muslim strongman in the employ of a Muslim organisation that usually hated all Hindus.

I hoped Avzal Bhai knew what he was doing, because I sure as hell did not.

We climbed a flight of stairs, each bowed and smoothed over time and on a narrow dark landing Avzal Bhai knocked on the door.

I heard the music even before the door was opened. A popular Hindi song from a few years ago played loud enough to seep through the thick wooden door and onto the landing outside.

The door was opened by a large woman, probably in her late 60s, wearing nothing but a skimpy *choli*[5] and a long skirt under it. She had her hair oiled and coiled sitting atop her head like a wound-up cobra. The rolls of fat, squeezed tight under her *choli*, hung over the top of her skirt, thick as Saraswati's rear tyres but nowhere near as firm, jiggling and wobbling around her waist as she stepped back to admit us.

Her face was thick with make-up: white powder under rouged red cheeks, a wide gash of red lipstick and her eyes encircled in a thick line of jet-black kohl.

Here was I thinking I was about to get a job.

---

5 A short, fitted crop top worn under a sari or over long skirts. Devised to turn the belly into a thing of beauty. Not always successful.

Looked more likely I was about to get an STD.

We walked into the central room of the establishment to find eight women, all dressed like their fat madam, either dancing to the music or lazing on the mattresses placed along the walls.

Some, through the magic of make-up, looked like schoolgirls.

Some, despite the magic of make-up, looked like headmistresses.

I suppose it depended on whether you felt like a wanking or a spanking.

'Welcome, Avzal Bhai,' gushed the madam, smiling wide to reveal red *pan*-stained teeth. 'Some pleasure before business?'

I have to tell you here, that like most men of my age, sex plays heavy on my mind. But I was overjoyed to see Avzal shake his head.

The artificial painted faces. The cheap, suggestive clothing. The oily hair.

The heavy stench of local perfume mingling with the incense burning in a corner.

Nothing there inspired even the slightest tingle of ardour.

Or perhaps, given my somewhat uncertain situation, the desire to survive just took precedence over the desire to have sex?

I quickly followed as Avzal walked through the room and down a corridor with several doors leading off it. I presumed these rooms were where the ladies entertained their clients. Bypassing them all, we turned a corner to be faced with a heavy metal grille guarding yet another door.

Avzal pressed a bell mounted to its side, and a large black eye peered out a peephole.

He then whispered to me out of the side of his mouth. 'Say nothing unless you are asked a question. Do not look into his eyes; look down at your feet. And no sudden moves,' Avzal concluded as the bolts behind the grille creaked open to admit us.

Nothing prepared me for the room we stepped into.

We had just walked past cracked and peeling walls painted in gaudy, mismatched colours. We had seen tattered mattresses and faded pictures hanging at uneven angles. We had breathed air that hung heavy with stale rose attar, sandalwood and sweat. We had trodden on cracked and broken tiles.

But the room we now entered would have put any five-star hotel to shame.

Pastel-coloured walls, blending perfectly with pale-coloured couches lining the walls. The furniture looked new and, to my inexperienced eye, not just Indian expensive but American expensive.

We walked in on a white carpet so thick I almost lost sight of the feet I had been commanded to stare at.

Heavy drapes covered the windows, wisely shutting out the scenic delights of Behndi Bazaar. Instead, table lamps spread low pools of light across the room.

The heavy odours of the outside world were chased away by draughts of cool air pumped down upon us from the ceiling.

To me, it looked like a room out of some fancy magazine.

But surprising as all that was, it was dwarfed by a large wooden desk, the colour of burnished mahogany, set into a corner of the room.

It looked as wide as a pavement and as long as a cricket pitch, the front of it ornately carved with forest scenes of elephants, deer and tigers all frolicking together as women carrying *matkas* of water on their heads walked past them towards a river.

Impressive even if not strictly zoologically feasible.

On top of the desk sat a single computer and a single phone, nothing else.

The polished bare expanse of wood shimmered under the light of a single desk lamp.

Imtiaz grabbed my arm and ushered me to a couch.

The couches, on which sat 15 other men, were set in a crescent shape to face the desk, like a small amphitheatre. The desk was obviously the focal point.

In front of the desk sat a single straight-backed visitor's chair with no arms and no cushions, as if the occupant's discomfort could only help expedite whatever business needed concluding.

Behind the desk it was a different story.

A large leather armchair, plush and imposing, its back turned to the room. Behind that, a wall-to-wall cabinet housing at the centre a TV, a stereo and a brightly lit bar with bottles I had never seen before. All around these items, from floor to ceiling were hundreds of books of all sizes and colours.

All signs of a man of taste and breeding.

Here, housed in this ramshackle building in the centre of one of Mumbai's most run-down suburbs was a room fit for a king.

Or, more correctly, the man who ranked just below king.

For, as Avzal Bhai walked up to the desk, the chair behind turned to face us all.

I had only heard stories about Sheik Mohsin, the MD of Bade Mian's large and sprawling organisation.

It is said that he had worked, fought, cheated, lied and killed his way from the very bottom to now hold the post of second-in-command to the big boss.

Nothing in the organisation happened unless Sheik Mohsin approved it.

No business deal took place without his blessing.

And no employee was hired until he personally approved it.

When I finally looked up from my feet to catch a glimpse of him, I was surprised by what I saw.

Most men who work for the organisation shared a common look.

Mean, scarred, cruel, battle hardened.

Sheik Mohsin looked like a youthful film star.

A shock of thick black hair, reddened with a little *mehendi* at the temples.

A well-shaped nose, straight enough to prove that no hand had ever lain a punch on it.

Eyes I can only describe as wise, and a fair and unblemished complexion with a perfectly shaped and trimmed beard nestling under it.

About him, an imperial air, just the right mix of authority and humility.

The very picture of a well-brought-up, well-educated Muslim gentleman.

He must be very sure of his position, I thought. In this business, only the very secure can afford to look as if they moisturise.

He could not have been a day over 40.

I was pleased, being just 19 myself at the time, at the prospect of joining an organisation that obviously believed in promoting youth.

As Avzal approached his desk, Sheik Mohsin sat back and pointed to the lone seat across the desk from him.

'All done?' he asked.

Avzal's tone of voice, so gruff and condescending with me, now changed to one that was deference itself.

'The matter was concluded successfully, boss. It will not resurface.' This said with a little smile.

Really, someone had to have a word with this man about his sense of humour.

'Good. Then we are avenged.

And who is this little pariah you have brought in with you?'

I looked up startled.

I had not realised he had noticed my presence.

Sheik Mohsin was looking down at his hands as he spoke.

But all the other 15 pairs of eyes were now trained on me.

'His name is Ricki. He helped me in taking care of business tonight.'

Sheik Mohsin, satisfied now with the state of his cuticles, looked up at me.

I saw for the first time that his eyes were grey. Cold and so pale they were almost see-through.

'Stand up, boy,' Avzal hissed.

I complied, trying hard not to let them see the tremble I could feel all over my body.

Mohsin looked me over from top to bottom. Then, he lifted his nose and sniffed the air.

'Gujarati, I think. I can smell the *methi.*'

I must admit that I was mighty impressed by this.

I always knew we Gujaratis had a bearing of our own.

I never realised we also had our own bouquet.

'I presume a Hindu!' he said turning to Avzal as if seeking an explanation for this unspeakable violation.

Unlike Avzal, I thought this man looked cultured enough to appreciate the literary brilliance of *Brother Brother.*

'Sir, I am both Hindu and Muslim.

I respect the optimism of the Hindus and the…'

'Shut up, cockroach!' barked Avzal Bhai.

'Any more of that nonsense and I swear I will personally make sure you never speak again!'

Mohsin turned his grey eyes towards Avzal.

'Why have you brought this urchin here? He looks too small to be useful and too stupid to be trustworthy.'

Sheik Mohsin obviously did not believe in the 'make the candidate comfortable' school of job interviewing.

Avzal, sitting on the little straight-backed chair, leant forward towards his boss as if about to share a confidence.

'Sir, I don't know how trustworthy he is, but if you don't like what I am going to propose, Imtiaz will take him out and kill him so he can't do us any harm.

He is small, but as I saw tonight, he can be quite resourceful.

He talks too much! But he can also think on his feet.

He needs to learn respect, and sir, yes, he is a Hindu.

But that is why I have brought him here. He could be useful. With your permission, Boss, I have an idea.'

Mohsin smiled. 'A useful Hindu? How intriguing.'

Avzal continued, 'Boss, how many years is it now we have tried to expand our business north of our traditional market? But that bastard Salgaonkar has eyes and ears everywhere. Every time we send in a sales team to persuade his distributors that our products are better in quality and value, Salgaonkar hears about it and our sales force...well...we never see them again.

Who knows what that dog does to them?

I think, the moment he hears there is an unknown Muslim asking questions or talking to his people, he thinks they come from us.

God knows how many innocent Muslims he has had killed just on the off chance they work for you.

Also, when we carry our products into his territory, if his men spot an unknown car or van parked near any of their establishments, he probably gets his tame police inspectors to check on the number plates. Anything registered to our organisation or even just in a Muslim name then gets followed, stopped and dealt with.'

At this point Avzal got up and walked towards me. He lifted me off the couch and held me out at arm's length like a fisherwoman holding up a day-old pomfret.

'But this fellow, this innocuous little boy, there is nothing threatening or unusual or even interesting about him. In fact who would even look at him twice?

What's more, if he were stopped and questioned, all he has to do is drop his pants and he would be clear of all suspicion.'

Avzal paused to let this point sink in.

The men all 'tsk-ed' and '*chi-chi'd*' as if disgusted by the very thought of what lay under my pants.

I gulped. Seldom can a foreskin have caused such foreboding.

Avzal continued on as if now delivering his master stroke.

'But best of all, sir, he has a rickshaw. He drives round Salgaonkar's territory all day. He has a legitimate reason to be there.

We make some adjustment to his rickshaw to enable it to carry our stock, perhaps under the seats, or hidden within the canopy and we have a delivery vehicle and driver Salgaonkar's men would not even look at.

Look at him, sir, who would ever believe this little runt of a *rickshawalla* would be working for us?'

He stopped, giving Sheik Mohsin the opportunity to muse on the proposition just put to him.

I must confess nothing he said did much to calm my jangling nerves or boost my confidence.

Runt, cockroach, innocuous, uninteresting?

They had better pay well, I thought, because the employee appraisals really were not worth taking home.

Sheik Mohsin rose from his chair and walked up to where Avzal and I stood in the centre of the room.

Not a man spoke. Not a throat was cleared.

Fifteen breaths were bated in anticipation of the judgement Sheik Mohsin was about to pronounce and, presumably, the entertainment to be had if it went against me.

Sheik Mohsin began a slow walk around me as if appraising the goods.

Avzal Bhai still had a firm grip on my arm so I stood still, facing the front the way our teacher at school made us do when we got the words wrong to our daily rendition of the national anthem.

I heard Sheik Mohsin's voice from behind me.

'You have a nice nose, boy,' he said in a gentle tone of voice.

At last, a kind word. 'Thank you, sir,' I said.

'So remember, if you let us down, if you cheat or steal from us, I will personally cut it off.'

His tone, so caring and courteous was hard to reconcile with the brutality of his message.

He had not yet finished.

'A rickshaw driver. So good eyesight then?'

'Yes, sir.'

'Excellent. Then keep in mind that if you ever disappoint Avzal Bhai, or show disrespect to any of the men here, if you ever deceive or double-cross us, I will have them remove both your eyes.'

I realised, with some relief, that we were now discussing employment terms.

'Are you man enough to work for us, boy?' he asked, his face now just a few inches away from mine. 'Remember, once you join us, you are here for life.

Serve us well and we can be extremely generous.

Betray us and we will be completely ruthless.

Do you understand?'

'Yes, sir,' I gulped, my fate sealed.

Well, they were hardly going to let me withdraw my job application now were they?

He turned to Avzal.

'Alright. He is your responsibility. Start him on something small and let me know how he does. But I want him watched day and night. He can move in with Imtiaz.'

With that, we were dismissed. He turned to discussions with the next man in line, and Avzal, Imtiaz and I left the room. We walked back out through the brothel, down the stairs and back onto the street.

There, Avzal lit a cigarette and leaned back against the jeep.

Imtiaz stood over my shoulder, my guard dog already at his post.

'Alright, boy, you have your wish. You work for me. You will drive your rickshaw as normal. Pick up passengers, go about your normal routine. From time to time, I will give you a parcel to deliver or have something for you to pick up. Whatever you make with your rickshaw you keep. Over that, with every delivery you make, you will get a delivery fee from me. Is that clear?'

I nodded.

He peeled notes off a wad of rupees and handed them to Imtiaz.

'Tomorrow, go buy him a mobile phone and some clothes. Make sure he is suitably dressed. As of now, and unless he fucks up, he is one of us.'

And that, friends, that one night of fear and confusion and opportunism is how I became 'Assistant Manager, Sales and Distribution, northern division' at one of India's largest and most brutal criminal organisations.

FIRST INTERMISSION

7

FAST-FORWARD TO THE PRESENT

Everything I have related to you so far happened seven years ago when, as I said earlier, I was just 19 years old.

I am 26 now.

The intervening years seem to have rushed by with the speed of the Punjab Mail.

In the early days, I drove my rickshaw all over Salgaonkar territory pretty much as I had always done.

Once every second or third day, I would get a call on my mobile, a number only Avzal Bhai knew, and be directed to a location where one of his men, usually Imtiaz, would be waiting for me.

He would hand me a brown parcel, sometimes as small as a single brick, sometimes as large as a loaf of bread. He would give me a name and address and a time at which the parcel had to be delivered.

He would also then hand me Rs 2000, my reward for being a faithful delivery boy.

It was beyond my wildest expectations.

Typically, keeping Saraswati on the road cost me about Rs 750 a day. This included Rs 140 for a tank load of gas and Rs 600 to Ram Lal Gopilal for vehicle rental and the auto permit.

This did not of course include unforeseen costs such as a flat tyre or a bent policeman.

On a good day, I took in Rs 900–1000 for 15 hours on the road. Which, after expenses, left me about Rs 200–300 profit a day or, if I worked all seven days, about Rs 2000 per week.

Avzal Bhai paid me that to make just one trip, usually lasting no longer than an hour or two.

On average, in those early days, I made Rs 6000 a week working as his own private courier.

The spending power Bollywood had initially enticed me with was beginning to be mine.

For the first time ever, I had money to spend on me.

It bought me new clothes, a watch, a transistor radio.

It bought me freedom to do the things I wanted to do.

It bought me rum from a glass bottle instead of rotgut from a plastic bucket.

It bought me the good, cloth-covered 100-rupee seats at the cinema rather than the cheap plastic ones right under the screen that I had been sitting in.

All in all, it bought me a new appreciation of life.

I wasn't just here to see out my days. I was here to enjoy them.

The downside was that I had to move in with Imtiaz and six of Avzal Bhai's other employees in a small two-bedroom apartment in Lower Parel.

I paid Rs 500 a week for my space in the apartment, a minuscule amount for the privilege of having a roof over my head in this sought-after area, even if we did sleep four to a room.

But the rental plan was not devised to make money.

It was based on assuring the organisation a degree of security.

By having the eight of us live together, constantly rubbing shoulders and aware of each other's movements, we were our own security detail.

If we noticed anything out of the ordinary with one of our flatmates; unusual behaviour, an unusual amount of spending money or a break from their daily routine, we were encouraged to report it.

If after a night at a drink hall, one of us was being indiscreet or out of line, the others were expected to drag the offender away and keep him isolated until he sobered up.

And of course, there being eight of us, we were less likely to be targeted by Salgaonkar's men.

We looked out for and after each other.

It was nice to be able to stretch out on a mattress rather than sleep curled up on the back seat of a rickshaw.

And I must confess an internal toilet did offer some advantages during the monsoons.

But in truth, I never got used to living in close proximity with seven strangers, especially the roaring farts that tore apart the silence of the nights (particularly Rashid and his beloved fried *dahl*), the snores and the sleepy mutterings.

Over time, seven of the eight of us developed a comfortable relationship with each other.

Occasional dinners together, visits to the movies, time spent chatting about the working day. My flatmates became friends.

Rashid and I in particular hit it off quite well.

His role in the organisation was Manager Documents and Identities.

I did not know myself what that meant until Rashid explained it to me one day.

In India today, one needs authenticated proof of identity for just about everything.

In the old days, all you needed was a ration card.

But these days you need authenticated ID to get driving licenses or death certificates, to open bank accounts, to obtain a passport, to get a marriage license and even, in this age of cross-border terrorism, to get an Internet connection.

To get your official identification one needed to produce one's birth certificate or parents' marriage license.

In a country of more than a billion people, an estimated 25% of whom have never been registered or recognized by their government or the law, where illegitimacy rates are high and the illiteracy rate hovers around 26% nationally, you can imagine that a large percentage of our population has never bothered with papers, certificates or documentation.

In the past, one managed somehow, but today, with the advent of the Aadhaar card, a nationwide ID card instituted by our government that is essential to procuring just about all essential goods or services, it is impossible to exist without the right documentation.

But not to worry.

Where there are those who are needy, there will be those who are greedy.

For a few rupees, services like the one run by Rashid will provide you with any form of identification required, from birth certificates, to voter's cards to graduate degrees, to driver's licenses to passports. In any name.

A new but highly profitable area of business for the organisation, he proudly told me.

Rashid and the others proved to be trustworthy companions. The one exception of course was Imtiaz, who remained isolated and secretive. He seldom came out with us, would frequently disappear on his own without any explanation and kept himself aloof.

Rashid explained that Imtiaz saw himself as Avzal Bhai's PA and, as such, on a higher social level than us.

This was borne out by the fact that Imtiaz was the only one amongst us who had the use of a company car.

Well, it had been a car years ago when it limped off the production line, but in this day and age, the Premier Padmini is more of a punchline in any joke about post-independence India.

Before we opened our doors to the world, car manufacture in India was limited to three marques.

Two of these, the Ambassador and the Triumph Standard were old, failed British disasters long discarded by the West, but standard issue on our roads.

The third, a hybrid based on an original European design was the Premier Padmini, or Pad as it was affectionately known. Small, boxy, a tiny 1100cc engine, four gears on the steering column, an advertised top speed of 130 kilometres per hour (descending Mt Everest) all built onto a narrow wheelbase.

As a piece of automotive engineering, it was an embarrassment.

Everything rattled. Nothing shut as it should. The clutch slipped. The engine ate oil. The boot lid never closed fully. The bonnet was almost rusted onto the body of the car.

However, as a symbol of Imtiaz's position in the organisation, it meant the world to him.

Touch his car and all hell would break loose.

I made sure I kept out of his way, aware as I was that his eyes always seemed to be on me.

He seemed to me a man who had turned suspicion into a way of life.

For the first year or so I worked for Avzal, I was purely a delivery boy. I asked no questions, showed no curiosity in the contents of the parcels, never turned down a delivery irrespective of what time I was summoned. I just made sure the goods got to their destinations untouched and on time.

As their trust in me grew, they added collection duties to my job spec. I would be directed to a source who would hand me a box to be delivered only to Imtiaz or Avzal Bhai.

At first, the boxes were small and quite discreet. With time, the boxes turned to bags, and the bags grew into suitcases.

Obviously a rickshaw with no passengers and a large suitcase strapped to the back seat would have caused some suspicion.

So, I devised a way to get over this. When given the address of the collection point, I would drive around the area at peak times when rickshaws were all busy and hard to find, until I was waved down by a desperate potential fare.

I would then apologise, saying I was about to go off duty and was in fact on my way to pick up a bag of my belongings to take home for the night.

It's quite amazing how agitated people get when someone they see as their social inferior turns them down.

How dare serfs and servants have lives of their own?

I was treated to threats, insults, entreaties even on occasion, tears.

Having let them play out their act for a moment or two, I would then graciously give in, offering to take them to their destination provided I could stop to pick up my suitcase.

No one ever said no.

No passer-by ever suspected a passenger riding a rickshaw with a suitcase on his lap. And no passenger ever suspected he may be carrying lakhs of rupees on his lap.

When Avzal Bhai heard of my ruse, he was tickled pink.

He laughed and put a hand on my shoulder.

'Perhaps we should call you Tricki, not Ricki.'

Luckily, it never stuck.

Although I never looked into the parcels or asked about their contents, I cannot pretend not to have known what I was carrying for the organisation.

Is it not a pity that a country such as ours, which history and circumstance have burdened with so much natural misery, would want to bring further misery upon itself?

The fact is, India today is the single-biggest heroin market in southern Asia. Caught as we are between the world's two golden triangles, Afghanistan, Pakistan and Nepal on one side and Myanmar, Thailand and Laos on the other, there is no more natural collection and transit point for Asia's supply of drugs.

But we are more than a conduit. We are also a ready consumer. Of the 40 tonnes of heroin produced in Asia, nearly 17 tonnes are consumed in India. Of that, 8 tonnes are imported from our neighbours and having taken our Prime Minister's exhortation to 'Make in India' to heart, a further 9 tonnes are manufactured locally.

Currently, there are close to an estimated 5 million and more Indians addicted to heroin and ironically, as university attendance rises in our country, so too the demand for hard drugs.

And they say education is the way forward!

I learnt all these details later in my career with the organisation, but even in the early days, I knew that I was delivering more than a box of *laddoos*.

I will save you all the usual protestations of 'I never forced anyone to take drugs, what people do is their own business, people should be responsible for their own behaviour', all the usual nonsense.

I did what I did for money, for the opportunity to climb the ladder of success, to improve my lot, to live the bravura Bollywood life.

As simple as that. Judge me any way you like.

The surprise to me was some of the locations to which I delivered the parcels.

There were, of course, the expected mix of bars, brothels, corner shops, *paanwallas* and disreputable characters who worked for the organisation as private entrepreneurs.

Outlets that for some reason could not or would not deal with Salgaonkar or Muslim-run businesses that simply preferred dealing with other Muslims.

But I also regularly delivered my goods to a small selection of chemist shops, some doctors' dispensaries, one or two large supermarkets and the security guards at large office buildings and luxury apartments.

Heroin may be the one aspect of Indian life that recognises no caste or social barriers.

Over time, as word of our supply chain and our better prices spread, our list of customers grew.

One day, about two years into my new life, I was summoned to meet Avzal Bhai.

Imtiaz and he were eating dinner at a well-known biryani restaurant in Grant Road.

I was invited to sit at the table, but no move was made to have me eat with them.

Avzal Bhai spoke first.

'We need to expand our delivery service, Ricki. You have done a good job, but demand is growing, and you alone cannot supply all our customers. We're going to have to find another way to meet demand.'

I wondered if there was a termination letter or, more realistically, termination bullet about to be delivered.

Imtiaz took up the tale outlining the problem they had obviously been tussling with.

'Trouble is, if our operation gets larger, if we start having our vans and our people moving around there, Salgaonkar will notice, and we'll be at war with him. That will not be good for business.

We need to be as discreet as we have been so far and still somehow service a wider area.'

There it was again.

After having lain low for a couple of years or so, she had turned up and tapped me on the shoulder once more. Fate, unannounced and unexpected, was opening another door. Was I up to the challenge of walking through?

So many people in our country believe that kismet or destiny is an end point that cannot be altered.

I believe it is a starting point.

Kismet is an opportunity presented, not a destination preordained.

It's about being present at the right time and in the right place.

What you choose to do with it then determines your eventual destination.

I cleared my throat and asked Avzal Bhai for permission to speak.

'Avzal Bhai, perhaps I can help you. Why don't you buy three or four rickshaws and hire three more drivers, and you will be able to supply more buyers the way we now do it.'

He shook his head. 'I cannot have my name or the names of anyone in our organisation involved. Salgaonkar will find out immediately. Besides, do you think I am some circus master looking after you and three other trained monkeys?'

OK. Now or never.

'In that case, sir, let me do it for you. Salgaonkar does not know me or that I work for you. We could start a small rickshaw company, with a Hindu name to make it even less obvious, and I will run it for you. I will find the drivers, make sure they are loyal and committed to us. Men who will ask no questions. You still control where and when the deliveries get made. I just keep the rickshaws rolling. In fact, you could make Imtiaz Head of Despatch so only he and you know the details of who we supply. He can instruct the drivers, give them the parcels. I don't want to know the details of your customers. I just want to keep the delivery service going for you.'

Avzal looked at Imtiaz searchingly and then back to me.

'What would it cost, starting this rickshaw company?'

'Well, sir, you can buy a good used rickshaw for about a lakh rupees. To own a rickshaw, we need an owner's permit. Officially, these are about Rs 20,000, but as there are almost no new permits being issued, you have to buy them from current holders. These can cost anything up to Rs 5 lakhs.

The rickshaw drivers will pay us Rs 400 a day to rent these rickshaws, so our business looks completely legitimate and they keep the rest of their daily take. You can decide what you want to pay them for making your special deliveries. There will be costs for registering the company and some running costs, but I don't know anything about that.'

I stopped here. I did not want to sound as if I was selling an idea. I wanted him to think that I, the dumb disciple, was just doing him another service.

He did the arithmetic.

'So, for about Rs 20 lakhs, we could have three additional rickshaws, plus yours of course?'

'Yes, sir,' I replied. 'And the company will earn about Rs 1200 a day from the three new rickshaws. So you will profit both ways, from the goods you supply and the means by which you supply them.'

He looked at me enquiringly.

'And you will run it? You will be responsible for the drivers, the vehicles and the business?'

'I know nothing about business, sir, but if you want me to, I will do it. I suggest we find a small office space or warehouse in Salgaonkar's territory and register the company there. In fact, I will move into the premises as so many start-up business people do to save costs. That way nothing ties me to the organisation, not even the apartment I am in (Rashid's farts were growing more rancid by the day). Imagine, sir, a part of our organisation, working in the heart of Salgaonkar country. What a triumph.'

The smile that spread across his face was all the reply I needed.

'I will speak to Sheik Mohsin. We have you, a *rickshawalla*, running a small rickshaw business. That makes sense. Imtiaz is our go-between. That makes it secure. And we have our first operational venture in the North. That would be a real business coup.

I like it. I think it could work.'

He looked genuinely pleased.

I tried to look humble and subservient.

Imtiaz looked suspicious and envious.

I realised that as I rose in Avzal Bhai's estimation, I would sink in his.

'OK, Ricki,' Avzal said, turning to me again, 'I will give you the answer in a day or two.'

I saw Imtiaz looking at his watch purposefully. My cue to leave, I thought, but instead, he turned to Avzal Bhai and said, 'If there is nothing else, Boss?'

Avzal Bhai just nodded, and Imtiaz rose, bade Avzal Bhai a courteous goodnight, grunted at me and left the table.

Avzal Bhai saw the surprise in my eyes.

'Don't worry, Ricki. Imtiaz is my most loyal employee, but he is first and foremost his own man. No one knows what he does or where he goes, but once business is done, unless I ask him to stay behind, his evenings are his own. I think he enjoys time to himself. He has always been a loner.'

'Has he worked for you long, Boss?' I asked.

'Since he was a boy. He never knew his mother. His father Imran, who raised him single-handedly, was one of Bade Mian's most trusted lieutenants. For years, they worked together, clawing their way up from the gutters of South Mumbai to get to where Bade Mian is now today. There was never any doubt that his son, Imtiaz, would follow him into the business.'

'Where is his father now?' I wanted to know.

Avzal Bhai sighed.

'Those were treacherous times, Ricki. There were several organisations fighting each other for power and territory. It was a constant battle to grow the business. His father, Imran, was Bade Mian's enforcer.

When someone in the opposition needed taking care of, Imran was sent to do it. His skills with a knife are legendary. Imtiaz learnt his craft at his father's knee. He adored his father.

When I joined the organisation, Imran was my first boss. He looked after me, taught me a lot.'

I knew there was more coming. Avzal Bhai looked like a man reliving a painful memory. I said nothing, waiting for him to collect himself.

'One day, Bade Mian sent Imran out to deal with a South Indian thug called Raghu Rao, who was trying to cut in on our territory. They were particularly nasty, these *Madrasis*. They pretend to be highly literate and cultured, but in truth, they are just greedy and ruthless. Bade Mian wanted to put an end to the threat before it escalated into a full-fledged war.

Imran had just taken delivery of a new car that morning. He was going to take Imtiaz and me out for a drive that evening, but wanted to attend to Bade Mian's assignment first. He drove off, assuring us he'd be back in a few hours.

A full day passed, and we heard nothing from him.

The next day Bade Mian sent every man out to look for Imran. We searched all the known areas that Raghu Rao hung out in. Every street, every back lane. It was I who found the car. It had been left by the railway tracks in Lower Parel. Unfortunately, Imtiaz was with me. There was no sign of his father. Everything about the car looked normal.

Then, we opened the boot.

He was a big man, Imran.

The bastards had sawed off his legs in order to stuff him in the boot. Not a great way for a son, 16 years old, to find his father.

The day after the funeral, Imtiaz came to tell me that he would be going away for a few weeks and I was not to go looking for him. I understood that he needed time to come to terms with what had happened. I wished him luck and told him to call me if he needed anything. He just shook his head and said that this was something he had to deal with on his own.

With that, he disappeared.

The first one they found was one of Raghu Rao's junior managers. His ears had been cut off and stuffed in his mouth.

A few days later the body of one of Rao's senior assistants turned up. He was missing his tongue and both eyeballs.

Then Rao's right-hand man, a nasty piece of work called Shiv Ram, was found floating in Pawai Lake. It looked like he had been filleted. No backbone.

Over the next week, three more of Raghu's men were found, sliced up with almost surgical skill. By now, there was real panic in what was left of Rao's gang. Several of his men fled back down South. Several more just vanished. As far as I know, to this day, none of them have reappeared.

Finally, one morning, they found Raghu Rao himself.

Well, not really him, just his severed head, hanging from the rear-view mirror of his fancy foreign car, like some sort of ornament. They never found the rest of him.

A few days later, Imtiaz reappeared. He told me he had made peace with himself and was ready to go back to work. I never asked him any questions. He never volunteered any information.

He only asked me if he could keep his father's car. That battered old Padmini Premier that he drives to this day. It's more than a possession to him. It's a shrine to his father's memory.'

'Over those three weeks, whatever happened or whatever he went through, turned him from a young, easy-going teenager into the hard, merciless man he is now.

That's why I say to you, Ricki, be wary of him.

He may look like a laughable figure but he is lethal.'

As I listened to his story, speechless and wide-eyed, the truth about my position started to dawn on me.

I had joined this organisation out of greed and a need to change the course of my life. It had seemed like an adventure, a little dangerous, a little risky, but exciting for that.

Avzal Bhai's story drove home the truth that what I had thought of as a game was, in fact, a bloody and brutal business run on the basic principle of an eye for an eye.

There would be no talking myself out of this.

No escape from the expectations this organisation placed on its employees.

I thanked Avzal Bhai for taking me into his confidence and was about to leave when, out of the blue, he handed me official notification of my promotion from apprentice to full-fledged, permanent employee.

'Sit down and have some biryani,' he said, chewing on a mouthful of rice and lamb. 'I think they have a vegetarian version for Hindus.'

As I ate with him and chit-chatted about trivial matters, I had to admit to myself that Avzal Bhai's story had driven home the truth.

I had sold more than just my services to this organisation.

I had sold my soul.

8

GATHER THE PROPS AND EQUIPMENT

The bright-blue board was raised by ropes and finally, after much shouting and directing from those assembled below (Avzal Bhai, Imtiaz, the head signwriter, three new drivers and myself) was affixed to the front of the warehouse.

Slightly off-centre and with one corner hanging a bit low, but that was to be expected.

All we Indians are natural experts in giving directions and emotionally incapable of taking any.

Finally, as it sat above the door to my new office, I was able to stand back and savour the bright yellow and red letters upon it:

SARASWATI TRANSPORT CO. Prop: R. Shah.

I cannot describe the pride that swelled in me.

I had a new business. A status in life. And a new name.

(Well, I wasn't about to upset Avzal Bhai by trashing the name he was so proud of, and anyway, Shah is a prominent

Gujarati name that, when seen on its own, was not an embarrassment.)

Sheik Mohsin had approved the plan, and in the two months since the biryani dinner, Avzal Bhai and I had gone about establishing the business.

Avzal wanted to know everything about owning rickshaws. He asked me who owned Saraswati and what made for a good business model.

I told him what little I knew about Ram Lal Gopilal.

He had just about everything we needed: four rickshaws, an owner's permit and a successful business, but he did not strike me as a man willing to part with any of it.

Avzal reminded me that acquisition and expansion was his department, not mine.

A few days later, as I drove Saraswati into Ram Lal Gopilal's compound, Avzal Bhai leaned across to me.

'Let me do the talking, Ricki. Just shut up and try to look tough.'

I was delighted at not having to negotiate with the fat Marwari who had been screwing me for a return well over the odds for some years now.

Avzal Bhai looked particularly impressive that morning in a white shirt open to his belly, sleeves rolled up to show his airbag-like arms, a red bandanna around his neck and of course, the gold chain shining against his hairy chest.

He was carrying a beaten-up brown satchel that gave him the air of a particularly unsavoury businessman, one whose negotiating tactics favoured the physical more than the verbal.

Ram Lal, no stranger to stand-over men and the protection racket, sized up the situation pretty much the moment he saw us walk up to him.

He tried claiming the upper hand with a bit of useless bluster.

'I suppose you have come to try and renegotiate the deal,' he said. 'I suppose you want me to lower the daily rate as times are difficult and gas prices are going up and this Uber-Shuber is taking more customers away. I have heard it all, and there will be no reduction in my charges.'

Avzal Bhai replied in a friendly, even conciliatory tone.

'We have nothing to negotiate, Ram Lal sahib,' he smiled.

'We are going to buy your rickshaws, your owner's permit and your entire business from you. We will pay you Rs 50,000 for each rickshaw and Rs 5 lakhs for the permits. I trust that is satisfactory?'

For the first time I understood the true meaning of buying power.

Ram Lal looked like he was going to burst. This was worse than he had imagined. His belly expanded even further, and his eyes looked as if they would pop out of his face.

'Thief! *Goonda*! You come here and try to bully me? I have seen a thousand like you. You don't scare me. Get out of here. Get out right now!'

Avzal smiled at him.

'If you insist. But first I have a message for you.

Madam Soonu said to tell you that your customary Wednesday afternoon arrangements have all been made and she looks forward to seeing you again.'

The man belched, his face turned purple and for a moment I thought he was going to puke. Then, slowly, he started to deflate like a *puri* that's just had a finger poked into it.

When he got his tongue working again, all he could do was stutter and stammer.

'Are you...you...you... trying to blackmail me? Are you threatening to ruin me?'

Avzal's smile now turned into a snarl.

'My partners and I do not threaten, Ram Lal. We act!

I do not want to ruin you. I do not want your wife to find out about Madam Soonu.

Nor do I want your little farm in your village near Nagaur to burn down.

Nor do I want your daughter Leelavati who teaches Hindi literature at the fancy college in Mumbai to fall out of the 7.45 a.m. Bandra local she catches every morning.

You have done very well out of your rickshaws, have you not?

You have your bank accounts in the Bank of Surat and Meena Bank, both very healthy.

You have that steel Godrej cupboard in the bedroom of your apartment in Andheri full of your...er...shall we say hard-earned cash?

You are a healthy, happy man of 80 years. Isn't it time you thought of retiring? You have no son to leave your business to. Leelavati's husband has a good clerical job in the Mantralaya. Surely it's time to take it easy?

After all, passing a successful business on to a new, younger generation is standard business practice in a patriarchal society like ours.

It's how we keep our country running, is it not?

Think of the Tatas, the Birlas, the Ambanis.

The older family members hand over to the younger members who bring new ideas, new energy, new excesses.

Wouldn't you like to add the illustrious name of Gopilal to that respected list of Indian business empires?

Perhaps they will name a hospital or concert hall after you.'

I must say I was impressed.

In a few days Avzal had put together a thicker dossier on the randy old crow than the income tax department would have put together in 50 years.

Why is Indian private enterprise always so much more enterprising than its government-run counterpart?

Ram Lal was close to tears.

'But, but…what you are offering is nothing. I have four rickshaws, and my business does well. How can I sell for what you are offering?'

Avzal switched back again to charm and generosity.

'Well, let's discuss what I am offering you.

A healthy life for the rest of your natural days, long may that be.

A trusting, contented wife.

A daughter who is safe and sound.

A son-in-law who keeps his job.

Your farm, your apartment, your Godrej full of black money and all your bank accounts.

On top of that, we are willing to be generous to a much-respected man such as yourself.

We will pay you...let me up the offer...25 lakhs for each of your four rickshaws, the owner's permits, the registration papers and all the books and business accounts; everything relating to your business.

Now you know that is more than it's worth, but my boss, Bade Mian, who you may have heard of, is keen to offer you the extra money as goodwill.'

Ram Lal visibly blanched, now that he knew who he was dealing with.

This was no negotiation. It was an ultimatum.

At his age, did he really want to take on the most power-ful criminal organisation in South Bombay?

Avzal continued in his most respectful tone of voice.

'Think carefully, Ram Lal sir. You know going to the police will end up costing you more. These days in Mumbai you can't get to see a sub-inspector for under Rs 10,000. And that's just the start. Then there is the Inspector, who has his Assistant Commissioner, who will bring in the Deputy Commissioner...it will end up costing you lakhs before they even consider doing anything.

Meantime, if the tax department find out your cupboard contains enough cash to allow you to deal with senior police officials, they will be deeply offended at being left out, and then God only knows how much they will want to keep you out of jail.

Would it be wise to incur all that cost, when you should be spending your money on yourself?

We are offering you the chance to go back to your village a successful hero, with plenty of money and a happy retirement.

Buy some land. Grow pumpkins. Become the village headman.

The air there is so much healthier for an old man than the smog and smell of the city.'

I must admit, the final veiled threat notwithstanding, the offer sounded good even to me. What a negotiator he was turning out to be.

He then finessed the deal with one last inducement.

'Finally, Ram Lal Gopilal sahib, my generous boss Bade Mian has instructed me to tell you that Madam Soonu will throw you a private retirement party like no man has ever enjoyed before, and from now on, whenever you holiday in Mumbai, she will offer you the services you like at a special 50% discount, as befitting a member of our 'Frequent Fornicators' loyalty program.

After all, you are now someone that my organisation considers a cooperative friend, and we know how to show our gratitude.'

An hour later, after Avzal had dried Ram Lal's tears, patted him on the back, poured him a saucer of tea and got his signatures on a number of papers he'd pulled out of his satchel, we drove off.

'Congratulations, Ricki,' he shouted at me over the noise of Saraswati's two-stroke. 'You now own a rickshaw business.'

I was intrigued.

'How did you find out so much about him so quickly, Boss?'

Avzal laughed.

'His son-in-law hates him. He called him a stingy old bastard who cheated him on his dowry. Promised him a motorcycle but gave him a moped instead.

For a few thousand he was only too happy to give us a rundown on the old man's habits, hoards and whores.

Being a local government clerk he accessed his Aadhaar card information for us. His banks, properties, his income tax statements that showed an annual loss.

Isn't our government wonderful, Ricki?

They get all our information together in one consolidated form so that anyone with a few rupees can easily and conveniently buy access to everyone else's private details.

What progress our nation is making!'

A few day later, we drove to an abandoned warehouse in Wadala.

'The old owners left in a hurry,' Avzal told me. 'This is your new office. See, it has a big enough compound to park the rickshaws, an office space in the front and a small apartment in the back. This is where you will work and live.'

Along with the office, I also acquired Mr Arif the accountant. He would do the books, I was told. I was to report all daily earnings and expenses to him, and he would look after all the paperwork, legal and illegal.

'So he will pay our bills and taxes for us?' I asked.

'Haven't you learnt anything, Ricki?' Avzal looked at me disappointedly.

'An unsuccessful businessman pays no tax and in India, being unsuccessful is the secret to running a profitable business.

Our arrangement is simple. On paper, legally, you own this business. Whatever money the rickshaws make, you and I share 50–50. And, I will raise your delivery fee from Rs 2000 a trip to Rs 4000.

However wealthy you become, Mr Arif will make sure you run at a loss.

It is a sign of the trust I place in you and the added responsibilities you take on. Because, be absolutely clear about this, you still work for me, and if one of your drivers fails us, a parcel goes missing, or he talks to Salgaonkar's men, Imtiaz will first slit his throat and then I will deal with you as I dealt with that Dehliwalla pig. You remember?'

I nodded nervously. Who wants a night of partying with Avzal Bhai by the Mithi River?

Over the next few weeks I went about selecting suitable drivers. Men preferably from around my own village, with valid licenses no matter how dubiously obtained, and all Hindus of course. Their main qualification had to be dumb obedience and an absolute lack of curiosity.

I wanted a docile, malleable workforce grateful for employment and happy to be exploited for a handful of rupees.

The very same qualities that has endeared our tireless Indian workforce to so many successful foreign companies.

I found one-legged Ganesh (luckily with a right leg intact as the only foot pedal on a rickshaw, a somewhat unreliable brake, is on the right); Shripal, the almost blind and drunk; and Mukhesh, the fecund, father of seven perpetually hungry children.

Men not many others would employ.

Mr Arif the accountant got the firm legally registered in its new name. The registration papers and the owner's permit were now made out to me, and I was officially the owner of Saraswati Transport Co., a four-rickshaw transport company.

I still drove Saraswati around as in the past but with one big difference. I gave up the khaki shirt and pants of a mere driver for the white shirt and trousers of an owner driver.

Don't be fooled by those who tell you colour means little.

It is my observation that in this world, the lighter you go up the colour spectrum, the higher you go on the social scale.

Another big difference was in my position within the organisation and my new-found earning power.

Between my share of the daily business take, what I made on the road with Saraswati and the increased delivery fee I was now commanding, I was making over Rs one lakh a month.

My 3 or 4 deliveries a week had risen to 8 or 10 as Avzal Bhai insisted only I should service his larger, more profitable clients.

'Change makes these men nervous,' he confided one day.

'They seem to like and trust you, so only you will make deliveries to them. Unfortunately, they do not believe in predictive stock models. They will call for new supplies only when they get close to running out, anytime night or day.

So be ready, Ricki. They are your primary responsibility.'

I settled into my new routine very quickly.

At 8 every morning my workforce of the lame, the blind and the hungover would hand over the company's share of their previous day's take.

Unlike other owners who ran two shifts of drivers, I gave them my three vehicles for the entire 24-hour period. That way, they had time to make an acceptable income for themselves while also making the deliveries Imtiaz ordered them to.

Then, from about 10 a.m. to 4 p.m., I would head out with Saraswati. It wasn't so much that I needed the extra money but the fact that I still loved riding the roads. I enjoyed my interaction with passengers, my daily inspections of the changing landscape of the city I loved, of the freedom I felt.

You see, from 10 to 4, I did not really work for the organisation; I worked for myself. For a few hours I was the boss of me. I determined what I did and where I went.

That worm that hated taking orders was still alive and eating at me.

Then after a short break, from 6 p.m. and often until midnight I delivered and picked up my precious cargo.

To Imtiaz's disgust, I no longer took my instructions from him, only from Avzal Bhai.

I was no longer Imtiaz's lackey but more and more being treated as his equal.

This further widened the rift between us.

'I don't trust you, cockroach,' he once told me. 'You may have fooled the others, but I know there is something about you that smells. Remember, I will always keep my eyes on you.'

More and more I knew that if I wanted to continue my climb up the corporate ladder, somehow this was a problem I would have to find a solution for.

But not even my concerns about Imtiaz took away from the joy of my new-found spending power.

Finally, a Bollywood-like life of indulgence was mine.

By my 25th birthday, I could afford to have stylish safari suits made for me by a proper tailor, so no longer did I look as if I had stepped into my big brother's clothes.

I could eat in fancy restaurants.

One weekend I even booked into a fancy hotel in Mahableshwar and walked around all weekend in a thick white bathrobe with soft, fluffy slippers on my feet. I must have cut quite a dashing figure because wherever I went in the hotel, people kept staring at me.

That is where I first decided to eschew forever my al fresco forays into the fields for the smooth, cool caress of porcelain.

I still believe the old ways are better, but I had money now.

I could stop caring about what ill effect my habits might have on other people.

I discovered the pleasures of a jacuzzi, a spa, an in-house massage service and joy of all joys, 24-hour-room service.

Nothing in this world beats the thrill of munching on a *masala dosa* at midnight.

I taught myself about the finer things in life.

I bought a laptop computer, a colour TV for my little apartment behind the shop, a bed with a proper mattress and even a small bathtub.

I paid an unlicensed plumber to tap into my neighbour's illegally installed water tank so I had hot and cold running water, day and night.

I learnt about the difference between desi whisky and foreign whisky.

I upgraded from unfiltered Indian cigarettes to filtered ones. King-size, of course.

And I started to read books. Gujarati translations of all the world's most famous authors.

Miss Agatha Christie, Miss Barbara Cartland, Mr Ian Fleming, Mr Arthur Doyle, Mr Charlie Dickens, all the classics, the great names of literature, even our own Mr Salman Rushdie who, I think, must be the cleverest of all as I found him the most difficult to read or understand.

I even watched foreign movies on my new DVD player.

American, European, Japanese, Chinese, anything with Hindi subtitles.

I have to admit though, they never really worked for me.

Lots of talking, crying, dying, no dance numbers and only one interval.

That's not a movie. That's just life.

No! Nothing to beat three and a half hours of solid Bollywood for me.

All these changes happened slowly, over the course of a few years of course.

Meantime, I continued to build my friendships with the people I delivered Avzal Bhai's products to. Salim the chemist on Godbunder Road, Khar. The supermarket near Santa

Cruz market. The hotel manager at the 4-star hotel in Juhu. The building supervisor of the large block of prestige flats on Pali Hill.

They saw me as a trusted business ally and occasionally, I was even invited into their shops or premises for a cup of tea and a chat.

Life was good, but even then I was growing more and more aware that my life was not my own. It belonged to Avzal Bhai.

How much longer would I continue to be one of life's employees? I wondered.

Would I ever again experience the sheer freedom of having to answer to no one but myself?

I pushed these thoughts as far back in my mind as I could.

Our organisation was not known for the generosity of its employee retirement plan.

Life is strange, is it not?

No sooner do you get what you think you need when you realise you've lost what you really want.

Would I ever be free of the organisation?

Ah well, as my grandmother used to say, you can't hurry destiny.

Fate had brought me this far.

May as well sit and wait until she decides to throw me another *jalebi*.

9

DELIVER THE DISHUM-DISHUM

As it was, fate was not yet ready to release me from the arms of my employer. In fact, she was about to make even greater demands of me.

It happened one night, about six months after we'd started the Saraswati Transport Company. I was fast asleep in my little apartment behind the office, visions of my delicious Deepika dancing before me when suddenly all hell seemed to break loose.

Someone was hammering on the front door with ferocity enough to deflate even the most ardent dreamer. I sat up and looked at the clock. 2 a.m. I shivered. This wasn't going to be good.

I slipped my feet into the tattered old rubber slippers under my bed and walked out of my apartment, through the office, to the front door.

I peeked out the glass panel on the side, and my heart took a leap.

There stood Imtiaz, fire in his eyes, stamping his feet impatiently and brandishing a two-foot long machete with an edge on it that looked as if it could cut through steel.

The reddish stains on it, glinting on what little moonlight there was, bore testimony to the fact that this evil-looking weapon had turned many a goat into a Goa curry (Goan purists may well purse their lips, but I work for a Muslim gang, so goat it is).

He was dressed in a green string vest, clearly selected to show off his taut, muscular frame. It looked as if he had oiled himself all over, his skin shining ominously in the darkness.

For an instant I toyed with the idea of refusing to open the door, but from the veins standing up on his neck, I could tell that the man would not be denied. He'd probably break the door down as a prelude to starting on my head.

I noticed then that his car was parked in the forecourt, and I saw my friend Rashid standing by it, waving at me. Three others of our organisation stood impatiently by the open back doors as if in a hurry to get somewhere.

Surely, I rationalised, if he was planning to slice and dice, he would hardly have brought party guests.

Tentatively, I opened the door, and he burst into the room.

I was wearing nothing but an old pair of undershorts and a T-shirt, my legs and arms on full display. He looked me up and down and his lip curled in disgust.

I freely admit I do not have what our film magazines term 'a heroic body'. In fact, if I were to stand sideways, you might struggle to see anybody at all. I am best described as sinewy rather than sculptured. No surprise there. I am built to lift watches, cameras and other goods of value, not weights.

Clearly Imtiaz was not impressed.

'You look like a dehydrated okra,' he sneered. 'Put some clothes on now! Avzal Bhai needs us.'

I scampered into the back, jumped into the trousers and shirt I had flung off the night before and returned to the office.

'Grab a weapon,' he shouted at me as he hurried back to his car, 'something useful.'

'Useful for what?' I wanted to shout back at him, and then I got a look at what the other four milling about the car were carrying with them.

One of them had a bicycle chain with a heavy weight hanging off one end of it. One had an axe. One held a chopped-down pitchfork, its tines as evil-looking as a serpent's fangs. But most frightening of all, Rashid held in his hand an old cricket bat that had a 10-inch spike driven through the back, its sharp end sticking out the face. It gave new meaning to the phrase 'puncturing the field'.

Clearly, I was meant to arm myself too. But here is the thing. I may lack scruples, but I also lack stomach.

I hate to hurt. The thought of drawing blood from another, slicing into someone's skin or pushing in an eyeball is almost as abhorrent to me as the thought of someone doing the same to me.

Despite all the promises I had made to Avzal Bhai when applying for the job, I could no more fight than fly, which ironically, is exactly what I did whenever I sensed any sort of fight coming my way! This was not the time, however, to air my views on the moral eminence of non-violence.

I looked around the office. I was not exactly spoiled for choice.

A stapler? I would prefer something that did not require me to get that close to my opponent, and going by past experiences, I would probably end up stapling my thumb to my forefinger anyway.

An old-fashioned fountain pen? Who ever heard of anyone getting nibbed to death?

A letter opener? So blunt, even envelopes laughed at it.

Then, my eyes fell on something I had inadvertently left there the previous evening. I had been tinkering with Saraswati's insides and had walked into the office with a wrench in my hand. I had left it on the desk while I went in to wash my hands.

It was about 18 inches long with a head large enough to grip a 3-inch nut. Stainless steel, robustly made with heft and weight. Perfect, I thought. Looks like it could do some damage but not so as I'd cut my own fingers off.

I ran to the car, jumped into the back seat with three of my colleagues and off we went, pedal to the floor, the Padmini shaking herself up to a dizzying 40 kilometres per hour.

We drove through Vile Parle and Andheri in near silence, until I could contain myself no further.

'Where are we going? What are we doing?'

Imtiaz grunted at Rashid who started to explain.

'Yesterday, one of our madams who runs a dance hall in Kurla was badly beaten up. Bade Mian abhors violence towards women, particularly towards our working girls, and wants the matter put right.

We found out that the perpetrator is a filthy dog named Shankar Shiwde, one of Salgaonkar's lot. Avzal Bhai has called him out. Man on man, no holds barred. The only rule is, no guns. That way the police don't interfere, and they leave us to sort it out between ourselves. To save face, Shiwde has to accept the challenge. Us versus them. We settle this once and for all. He has to be brought to his knees, despatched in front of his men as a warning to the rest of those Salgaonkar snakes.'

My heart, already fluttering with the thought of the damage these weapons could do, now sunk to my boots.

We were expected to fight, hand-to-hand, in the dead of the night against an enemy who had been forewarned and, presumably, forearmed.

'How many of us are there?' I asked, trying desperately to keep the terror out of my voice.

'We six and Avzal Bhai,' Rashid replied.

'So seven against seven?' I asked.

The five of them burst out laughing.

'You think we're going to play netball?' Imtiaz asked, looking over his shoulder at me scornfully. 'I expect they will have at least a dozen. That means we will have a bit of fun tonight!'

I sat back, mind awhirl. How the heck was I going to get out of this? If I ran, Avzal would have his men find me and turn me into chutney. If I stayed, I had no doubt I'd be the first to fall, probably with a dagger in my chest. Neither option suited me particularly well.

I was turning all the possibilities in my mind as we turned off SV Road on to Perry Road and then right on to Carter Road. We drove past the railway colony and continued towards the fish market at Danda. Then, just before the road curves right again towards Khar, as we drew alongside the heart of Chuim village, Imtiaz slowed the car down and stopped on the verge.

Do you know that top end of Carter Road? If you face the fish market to the north, you have the ocean on your left. Between the road and the ocean stand a series of large bamboo frames, some 15 feet high and 20 feet wide. In between the two uprights, the local fisherfolk run ropes and thinner bamboo poles on which they hang their catch to dry under the relentless Indian sun. Bombay Duck in season and any other malodorous fish you can think of can all be seen shrivelling there, permeating the air with that pungent, gagging smell that only rotting fish can give off. On the other side of that road, to your right, you will see what looks like a wall of tenement houses. I have been told that once, the area there was an open field. But in time as our population grew, so too did the need for shelter, and the roadside was claimed by our more enterprising homeless, who had built an array of huts, shacks and makeshift homes. In time, these temporary structures were reinforced with wood, corrugated iron, even bricks. Doors and windows appeared, upper stories were added, TV antennas and air conditioners sprouted on rooftops as clandestine cables, snaking surreptitiously into the municipal electric lines, lit these homes with the unmistakable light of permanence.

A sea view, no land tax, and no municipal ordinances quickly turned these slums into select residences, much in demand.

Don't be surprised.

Survival is the art of turning nothing into something, and we Indians are expert at it.

Looking at this wall of houses and you would think the open field that once lay there was lost forever.

But never trust appearances in India. For, if one looked closely, tiny passages had been created between some of these houses, too narrow for the passer-by to notice, but strategically placed to allow the residents access to the fields that still lay there behind their houses. The residents had created a fortress, ringing the open field with their dwellings, thereby assuring themselves a huge, private backyard, their own soccer field, meeting space and cricket pitch.

The six of us walked through one such passage to find Avzal Bhai waiting for us at the end of it. While Imtiaz was as pumped up as a tiger on testosterone supplements, Avzal was as cool and collected as I have ever seen him. The prospect of blood obviously soothed him.

He wore a knuckle duster on the fingers of one hand and carried an evil-looking tandoori skewer, flame-hardened steel, some three feet long, in his other hand. The chef had come ready to tenderise with one hand and impale with the other.

He spoke to us in hushed tones.

'That bastard Shiwde and his men have gathered at the rth end of the field. We will approach them from the south. Do whatever you like to them, but remember, Shiwde is mine! You will know him from the orange trousers he is wearing. Leave him to me.'

With that, Avzal led us out of the narrow passage onto the field where he and the others strung out to form a line. I scampered about, uncertain of what to do or where to stand and decided that standing immediately behind Rashid, who was about seven feet tall and five feet wide was probably a strategically sound vantage point.

We watched as Shiwde and his men, about 11 of them by my count, assumed a similar formation some 200 yards away at the other end of the field. For about 30 seconds nothing happened. We just stood there and stared at each other, baring teeth and brandishing our weapons of destruction.

Apart from us gladiators, the field was deserted. The local residents had moved up to the windows on the top floor of the houses that ringed us. There they gathered, excited and eager for action. Peanuts were being passed around, and the *feni* flowed. Betting slips were exchanged and sides taken. Nothing excites the Indian public more than the prospect of free entertainment, and one that promised blood, bone and a body or two surpassed anything the IPL could ever offer. There was a perceptible murmur of anticipation that was silenced immediately when Avzal Bhai raised his skewer and shouted out loud, *'Maro sale ko,'*[6] and we were off, charging rapidly at our enemy as they, simultaneously, ran at us. Being a considerate man, I decided it was best I run some six

---

6 Indian version of 'kill the bastards.'

feet behind Rashid, so as not to trip him accidentally. The others were so blinded by their bloodlust, no one took notice of where I was.

Like two marauding forces, carried on the wings of vengeance, we ran towards each other, screaming and shouting, when suddenly I felt the ground disappear from under me and I sprawled forward onto the muddy earth, splattering myself with the oozing sludge into which I had fallen.

I looked about in surprise and then around me where I saw the fickle foot of fate that had come to my rescue.

My trusty rubber slippers, perfectly serviceable within the undemanding confines of my bedroom, were obviously not up to the wear and tear of warfare. The toe strap on one had popped out of the sole, causing my foot to slide forward and tripping me up ignominiously.

Having worked that out, I lifted my head to survey the scene in front of me. Pitched battle had begun.

A quick glance showed me that Rashid had embedded the spike on his bat into the thigh of one of the opposition who, not surprisingly, had lost all interest in ongoing engagement.

Latif, the combatant with the bicycle chain was waving it madly over his head, like the rotors of a helicopter and thereby keeping at least three of our foes at bay.

Imtiaz was slashing away with his machete and had already, from what I could tell, inflicted considerable damage to the shoulder of one of the opposition. So too, my colleagues with axe and pitchfork seemed well in control of affairs while Avzal and Shiwde, a little to one side of the throng, were fencing furiously, Avzal with skewer and Shiwde with a sharpened cricket stump.

Clearly, our guys had opened well, and the runs were coming nicely.

Now, this may surprise you, coming as it does from a self-confessed lowlife like myself, but I have always believed in fair play.

I absolutely abhor kicking kneecaps in kabaddi, or using double-tibble *manja* in kite fights or sandpaper on cricket balls.

I may be a scoundrel, but even a scoundrel has standards.

How unfair would it be, I asked myself, how unsporting if I was to join a fray so evenly matched and in so doing, tip the balance in favour of one side?

I may be a thief, a dealer, a cheat and knave of the first order, but I am not an Australian cricketer. I do have some moral standards.

Therefore, it's probably best if I just stay out of it, I thought to myself.

I realised though, having decided to hold myself back for future engagements, that I could not simply lie there in the open to be found by Avzal Bhai and thereby lose, in quick succession, respect, status and life.

Looking around me desperately, I noticed a narrow passage between two houses, a gap no wider than a man's shoulders, running off to my left. In an instant I was up, slippers abandoned, and into the passage, out of my colleagues' view and my enemies' strike range.

There I stood, flat against the wall, listening to the sounds of battle.

There were shrieks and shouts, groans and moans, blood-curdling screams and, from the spectators safely ensconced behind their windows, cheers and exhortations. From time to time, I would peep around the corner to check on proceedings.

Clearly, we were on top. Three of the opposing eleven were on their backs, seemingly comatose and of no further military use.

Two were nursing wounds that gushed red, both retreating hurriedly, showing no desire to stay around for post-match interview. Three more were surrounded by five of my colleagues and appeared to be in the process of attempting to negotiate an armistice. Three others were still on their feet, but the result was obvious to all. Only Avzal Bhai and Shankar Shiwde were still hard at it, skewer to stump, jiggling about like two Olympian fencers keen to make the first touché.

Shiwde, preoccupied though he was with trying to avoid a new life as a *chicken tikka*, had seen enough around him to know that no tail-ender, last-man heroics was going to save the match.

With a sudden lunge, he pushed Avzal to the ground and started looking around for the nearest exit. He started to run away from the action.

I immediately retreated back into my safe little niche to await the final trumpet call of victory. Best not to distract the boys when things were going so well.

I stood there, flat against the wall, when, to my surprise, I heard what sounded like scrabbling feet.

I pushed myself away from the wall and leant forward to peek around the corner, when suddenly a large, sweaty body in a blur of orange tore around the corner at breakneck speed and ran straight into me, his face hitting my forehead with the force of a cannonball.

Many may not believe this, but there are innumerable advantages to being short, one of them being that when taller men run into you, their noses, soft and squishy, make contact with the hardest, strongest part of your body; the forehead.

I heard a crunch, and suddenly, I was blinded by warm, gushing liquid that flowed over my face, and all down my shirt. When I could open my eyes, I almost fainted at what I saw in front of me. Standing there, stars in his eyes, his nose now pushed flat to one side of his face and blood pouring out of his nostrils was Shankar Shiwde himself.

It took a second or two for him to realise what was happening, and then the pain hit him. With a howl of anguish he dropped his cricket stump, his hands flew up to his face and he started to lower his head rapidly, bending forward in pain.

As he did so my arms, with no thought but self-preservation in mind, flew upwards to shield my face from possible retribution. These two actions, him bending double and me raising my hands as quickly as I could, took place simultaneously and, sadly for him, on the same trajectory. At some pace, the head of my 18-inch wrench caught him right between the eyes, straightening him up again. He looked at me in mute surprise for a second or two; then his eyes crossed, his knees give way and he crumpled before me, unconscious before he even hit the ground, face forward, his head between my feet.

I stood there stunned and terrified, my brain whirling. I could not move. What should I do? Where could I run to?

Where to hide? Before I could get out of there, I heard more running feet, and almost immediately Avzal Bhai and Imtiaz came flying around the corner.

They stopped in amazement at the sight before them.

Little Ricki Shah, barefoot, covered from face to waist in blood and mud and slime, wrench in hand with the leader of the opposing forces lying prone at his feet.

They looked at me, then down at Shiwde. At me, then Shiwde. Finally, Avzal put two and two together.

'Well done, Ricki, you got the bastard! Looks like you had one hell of a fight,' he added, looking at the blood still dripping off me.

Thank God Avzal could not add.

I may not be, as I have openly admitted, a man of action, but I know when to act.

'He was trying to run away from you, Avzal Bhai. He thought he could escape through this passage. I ran after him, and he set upon me. He's a big fellow, but...well...he won't be going anywhere for a while,' I panted breathlessly. I have seen boxers interviewed after a big fight, and they all pant. I did the same. I puffed and huffed like a man who had just gone through 15 high-energy rounds. Periodically, I thumped the head of my wrench into my palm as if to suggest I actually knew what to do with the darn thing.

'That should teach him some manners,' I said, bobbing around on my toes and rolling my shoulders as I have seen those boxers do.

Avzal bought every bit of it.

'Shabash, Ricki! I didn't know you had such fight in you. What an asset you've turned out to be. Well done! We could certainly use someone like you when we have these little skirmishes, right, Imtiaz?'

Imtiaz looked like thunder. I doubt he believed my story, but he was not going to correct the boss. He just had to suffer the mortification of watching any glory he may have dreamt of for himself being conferred on someone with the backbone of a newt.

My colleagues, when they caught up with us, were as impressed by my performance as Avzal Bhai. Listening to them, it became obvious that I was a shoo-in for the Man of the Match award.

'What a fighter, Ricki.'

'You got their main man.'

'Apna wrench-walla warrior.'

'You are a *bada* peg in a *chotta* peg glass.'

'Half plate Hercules.'

I was of course, grace itself, making as little of the praise as I could.

After all, we farm folk know that when one spreads manure, it is best to do so modestly, lest someone gets a whiff of too much shit in the air.

I cannot describe the relief I felt that it was over and I had come out of it reputation and body intact. But my joy was short-lived. Avzal Bhai had one more nasty shock for me.

He took the machete from Imtiaz's hands and held it out to me.

'Here, you get the honour. You caught him, so you gut him.'

The others all gathered round, eager to attend the grand opening of Shankar Shiwde's abdomen.

My brain raced furiously. As you will have gathered from what I said earlier, there is no way I could slice open a man. Apart from not having the nerve for it, chances are that the first sight of his viscera would probably have me falling down in a faint, thereby ruining my new-found reputation as Warrior Warlord, Pride of India.

Luck, in the shape of a busted slipper, had come to my aid once. I could not depend on her again. This time, it was all up to me. How could I mete out the punishment Avzal Bhai expected to see and, at the same time, not have to take a man's life?

I raised the machete high as if to plunge it into his chest, then stopped, mid plunge.

'It almost seems as if we are being too kind to him,' I said looking up at Avzal Bhai.

'What do you mean?' he asked angrily. Kindness was not a quality he approved of.

'Well, this dog is unconscious. I kill him now, and he feels no pain, no humiliation, no remorse. I'd rather make him suffer a bit.'

Avzal Bhai approved of suffering. 'How?' he asked.

'Well,' I replied, scratching my chin, 'the biggest punishment a man like him could suffer is total loss of face. If all these villagers started to laugh at him, if his men saw him in the most awkward, embarrassing light possible, that would be the end of him.

Not only could he never show his face again, he would probably have to run away from Mumbai to escape

Salgaonkar's wrath. After all, we not only make a fool of him, we make a fool of Salgaonkar and his whole gang.'

My colleagues nodded in understanding. Nothing determines one's stature in a criminal organisation more than the fear and respect one engenders. When your men, your enemies, the people around you lose that fear, you may as well pawn your gold chain, discard your daggers and go get a government job. You will never be respected again.

'So, how do we do that?' Avzal asked, now more than a little interested.

'My suggestion is, we strip him naked, then hang him upside down among all the rotting fish on the drying racks by the roadside. Tomorrow morning, every villager here, everyone who drives down Carter Road and all his own men will see Shankar Shiwde tied to the bamboo posts, his manhood on display, a minnow hanging among the mackerels. He will be the laughing stock of all Bandra, of his entire gang. Salgaonkar will never forgive him. If they allow him to live, he will be ruined. More importantly, what a slap in the face for Narendra Salgaonkar.'

One by one, as my colleagues started to visualise Shiwde and his squashed nose, hanging on the drying racks, naked and sautéing alongside the other seafood there, they started to snigger and then laugh out loud.

Even Imtiaz had to fight to keep the smile off his face.

'How cruel you are, Ricki. No man should have to suffer a fate like that. I like it,' said Avzal, chuckling to himself. 'I shall tell the residents here that no one from this village should cut him down. That way, he'll hang there until well after mid-morning. All of Bandra West will see him. OK, do it, Ricki.'

So the boys stripped him, Rashid carried him to the drying racks and we strung him up, tying his arms and legs to the bamboo poles. He swung there in the breeze like a giant manta ray, exposed to the sun, the sightseers and the sniggers of one and all.

Humiliation beyond human tolerance.

I don't know what happened to him the next day, who cut him down, but we heard that Shiwde, once released, made straight for Dadar station and caught the 3.45 express to Pune. From there, he beat a hasty retreat to his village near Sholapur, a good 450 kilometres from Mumbai, distant enough to evade Salgaonkar's wrath.

He was never seen in Mumbai again.

Avzal Bhai rang me the following afternoon.

'Bade Mian was very pleased to hear about the punishment you dished out. I am to reward you for your imagination and promote you. Well done, Ricki. At this rate, you'll be running your own team of men soon! Perhaps even have your own territory.'

I had wanted to cut ties with the organisation.

Instead, it sounded as if I was in the running for Employee of the Year.

Fate, what a fickle friend you can be!

10

WEAVE IN THE TWIST

One morning, soon after my 26th birthday, Avzal Bhai dropped into the office just as I was about to head out on Saraswati. Imtiaz tagged along behind him, a black face signalling his displeasure at being there.

'Ricki, we have an opportunity I want to talk to you about. You know about Bollywood, don't you, with all the movies you go to?

Have you heard of Glorious Cine Studio in Dombivili?'

I could not believe my ears.

How often in my early days had I hung off the gates at that very same place, hoping for a glimpse of my beloved Deepika. How many hours had I spent trying to peep over its walls.

One day, I even managed to make a tiny hole in the wire fence at the remotest corner of the site only to be chased off by a lathi-wielding guard.

Glorious Cine Studios was a mecca for us Bollywood dev-
otees. It's where you hung about not seeing the biggest stars
in India.

'I think I have heard of it, sir,' I replied.

'I have a major client there. More than that, he is a personal friend from the old days. We grew up together in Nulla
Bazaar. He is a valued customer, but at the moment he is
the only customer there. I have heard that some 2000 people work on that studio lot. Imagine the business potential.
Nervous, highly strung creative people. The perfect market
for us. If we crack it, we could make a killing there.'

Ignoring the obvious poor choice of words, I nodded
without interrupting. I really liked where this was going.

'Until now, I have had Imtiaz personally deliver our goods
to my friend. But Imtiaz lacks the...eh...sales patter that comes
so naturally to you. He scares people away. Imtiaz is my attack
dog. You are the friendly puppy people find irresistible.'

At this, the attack dog glowered, and I knew our enmity had
just deepened further.

'So, I want you to personally handle my friend's needs.
Get close to him. Meet others in the studio, and then, find a
way to expand our sales there. My friend is expecting you and
has agreed to introduce you to people. In exchange, we will
now extend him our 25% favoured-customer discount for all
his personal needs.

Look after him, Ricki, whatever he needs. Keep him
happy. Keep him safe. Are you clear about all this?'

I nodded almost in disbelief at the turn this road had taken. Was I finally to rub shoulders with film-makers and movie stars?

Is this where I meet the young starlet who would give up her rocketing career to become my devoted co-star in life?

I tried hard to keep a lid on my elation.

Best not to burst into song yet while these two were watching, I told myself.

'Here is the first delivery my friend needs.' Avzal motioned to Imtiaz, who grudgingly handed me the package he'd been carrying.

'At the studio gates is a security guard named Krishna. You will need to get past him, but I am told he is a very patriotic Indian.

Get him to direct you to Studio 6, and there, ask for production assistant Miss Kalpana. She is expecting you around 7 p.m. Don't fuck this up Ricki. If all goes well, this could mean a major promotion for you.'

At this, I thought I heard a little growl from Imtiaz, but nothing could dim the elation bubbling up within me.

That evening, having got into my newest safari suit with extra-wide lapels and shiniest mock-ivory buttons, I pomaded my hair as never before, exchanged my rubber slippers for my leather sandals and Saraswati and I started off for the studio.

I drove to the gates where a portly, officious man in an ill-fitting security guard's uniform stopped me.

'Where do you think you are going, *chintu*?[7] We don't allow riff-raff into this place. Come on, beat it.'

His name tag told me that this was Krishna, the self-important patriot I was to win over.

'Gandhiji said that as Indians, it is our duty to help each other at all times,' I replied, casually pulling a picture of our beloved Mahatma from my pocket. I always thought he looked particularly humble printed against the magenta background of our Rs 2000 note.

Krishna's eyes bulged at the sight of my offering. 'Is that right?' he gulped.

'Oh yes, sir. In fact, I think he said it twice,' I continued, pulling out a second slice of magenta magic.

Krishna slipped the father of our nation into his pocket.

'Where do you want to go, sir?' he asked now with a smart salute and big, deferential smile.

See, that's what I love about bribery.

It energises the receiver while elevating the giver.

A complete win-win!

Studio 6 lay at the very far end of the lot, a good kilometre or so away from the security hut at the entrance. I drove Saraswati up to a large sliding door. A bright-red light flashed above it and next to it a sign warning visitors not to ring the bell when the light was flashing.

So of course, I rang the bell.

I know this confuses visitors to our country but in India, signs are not to be taken as instructions to be obeyed but rather as invitations to be considered.

---

7 Hindi for 'short arse.'

So a 'Form Queue Here' sign is often where you find the greatest knot of humanity clamouring to get on the same bus at the same time.

The site of an 'Exit Only' sign is usually the most-favoured point of entry.

And the ubiquitous 'Please No Honking' sticker is simply a request to show your support for the wondrous qualities of silence by blowing a long, loud burst of agreement on your horn.

It's not that we are disobedient. It's just that we are disbelievers.

How can mere words ever improve the human condition when 14 successive prime ministers, 21,547,845 government employees, a police force of 1,926,000 and 82,237 newspapers raging daily about the state of the nation have failed so spectacularly to do so?

No. Best we just make our own decisions about what's right and proper.

The large sliding door finally swung open, and a red-faced young man with a walkie-talkie at his hip and a clipboard in his hands glared at me.

'Did you not see the sign about the red light?' he demanded.

'Yes, sir, I did,' I smiled back.

'Oh!' he exclaimed, taken aback by my ready admission of guilt. 'Well, luckily for you it is not working. It is stuck on red, and we were not shooting when you rang.'

Oh, India, I love you.

'I have a delivery here for production assistant Miss Kalpana,' I continued.

He looked me up and down, no doubt impressed by the safari suit. 'Wait here,' he commanded with all the authority ordained by a hardcover clipboard. I stood at the door, craning my neck to see inside.

It was a like a dream world to me.

Large circular lights stood on long stands, each beaming down with the brightness of the sun itself.

Shiny silvery boards shimmered under the lights, casting pools of sparkling, dancing shapes into the corners of the studio.

The clatter of people who were pushing around what looked like a balsa wood castle, each shouting instructions to one another.

Around them dozens more raced around, gazing into light meters, talking into their walkie-talkies and generally creating the impression of much effort and no result.

Clustered round a camera were a number of cloth chairs where the bosses sat, no doubt deeply absorbed with planning shots and rewriting scripts. At the moment they were deeply absorbed in the plates of *batata wadas*[8] sitting before them.

I breathed it all in with relish. I could smell stardom in the air.

But instead of the ravishing young bikinied starlet of my dreams, a dark-skinned, bespectacled, sari-clad woman of about 30 walked towards me.

---

8 A Mumbai must have! Blobs of potato coated and fried. The snack that clogs the arteries of a nation.

She was slim, of slight build and, miracle of miracles, shorter than me.

It's not that she was ugly. In fact, she had a pleasing face, oval in shape, with interesting features. Nice eyes, a nose that sat just right over two well-shaped lips.

It was just that she was no Deepika. Not even a Pinky Pal Kumari.

I tried not to show my disappointment over the discovery that here in heaven they also had mortals in attendance.

'Yes,' she asked, 'what is it?'

'I have a delivery for production assistant Miss Kalpana.'

'That's me,' she replied, looking me up and down. The safari suit was really paying off, I thought.

I held out the parcel I was holding. 'This is for you.'

She glared at me and took a step back in disgust.

'Don't you dare hand me that filthy thing. You think I would ever stoop to that level? It is the devil's business you do, and I want nothing to do with it!'

I stood there, confused, uncertain of what to do next.

She let out a deep sigh and shook her head as if matters were beyond her control.

'You had better come with me. You can give him that poison yourself!'

With that she turned and walked along the studio wall where a short staircase led up to a small mezzanine office.

'Come on,' the woman called out to me curtly, 'he hates to be kept waiting.'

I followed her up the stairs to a door. The sign on it read 'Private Office. Production Personnel Only'.

She opened the door, and we stepped inside only to be met with an angry roar of disapproval.

'Why have you brought him here?' a deep voice shouted at the girl. 'You think I want strangers here in my office? You think private means you can drag in any little shrimp you fancy? I asked you to bring me the delivery, not the delivery man, you stupid girl!'

I could not believe his rudeness. How could he talk to a young woman like that?

Amazingly, she started shouting back at him in an even louder voice.

'You old fool. I told you, I want nothing to do with this filthy business! I will not touch it. I will not encourage it. I will not condone it. How you kill yourself is your own business. Just do it quickly so I can be rid of you once and for all'

With that she turned and stormed out of the room.

I sensed immediately they were not friends.

Hostility like that can only mean one thing.

They were family.

11

GIVE THE HERO A SIDEKICK

I looked around the bleak little room as an uneasy silence descended upon it.

A table, desk, filing cabinets, large floor-to-ceiling safe, tray with bottles of alcohol, a small bar fridge. Other than one long couch placed against a far wall, it was an impersonal workspace, nothing more.

On one wall, large windows looked out onto the studio floor below, a perfect spot from which to see the action taking place there.

On the other, a single smaller window revealed a view of the studio car park where I had left Saraswati waiting for me under a large banyan tree.

I decided I had better try and smooth the waters.

'I am no stranger, sir,' I said, 'I have personally been selected by your old friend Avzal Bhai to deliver this parcel to you with all his salaams and respect. He wants me to service all your needs from now on, sir, day or night. That way, the matter stays private between us and no one else, like that... eh...angry young lady, need be involved.'

He looked a little calmer now.

Hurriedly he unwrapped the parcel I had laid on the table.

'Yes, she is rude. She gets it from her mother.' He turned to look at me closely. 'What is your name?'

'Please call me Ricki. And may I say, sir, what an honour it is to meet you. I have long admired your talent. In fact, you are my favourite star of all times.'

Sometimes a lie soothes better than the truth ever can.

And it was not all lies. For before me stood none other than that megastar of a decade or two ago, Bunty Bhaskar himself.

You may recall I mentioned him at the start of this story as a great star who 10 years ago was still playing lead roles well into his 50s.

Well, he certainly could not have played them anymore.

Time, or more probably his recreational preferences, had not been kind to him.

The bags under his eyes appeared to be racing each other to see which would reach his chin first.

His cheeks, sunken and gaunt, flapped when he talked like two sails in a weak wind.

His neck was lined with folds of loose skin like the defeated wattle on an ageing rooster.

He still had a thick head of hair, but the jet-black locks of yesterday were now as white as Himalayan snow.

The only thing untouched by time was that deep mellifluous voice that had made him the heart-throb of millions of women across the country.

'Another adoring fan I take it?' he asked, raising an eyebrow at me.

Obviously age had done nothing to diminish his arrogance.

'The biggest possible fan, sir. *Mr Detective, The Power of Love, Family Man, Angel of Love, A Man of Honour, Policewalla Number 543, Inspector Dalip,* and a *Fool in Love.* I have seen them all, sir.'

Well, I had not actually seen the last one thanks to Avzal Bhai's untimely intervention if you recall, but I have found that flattery and veracity do not always sit well together.

He smiled at me, his mind now cast back to the past, remembering a time when he was a god amongst actors and the hero of his age.

He was now ripping at a small plastic bag he had pulled out of the outer wrapper.

'You have a favourite I suppose?' he asked, wanting to hear more. Sad isn't it? How readily our bodies age and how steadfastly our vanities refuse to.

'So many great roles, sir,' I replied. 'So hard to choose. But if there is one I love to watch again and again, it is *Man of Honour.* The way you avenge the death of your wife and child; the courage, the power, that incredibly dramatic end scene of death and mayhem. And what wonderful dance numbers. It still makes me shiver when I think of it.'

By now he had torn open the plastic bag and laid out a clump of white powder on the table. Using a letter opener he cut the powder into two fine lines and, lowering his head, inhaled a line into each nostril.

'Ah yes,' he nodded, sniffing and inhaling deeply. Powder hung around his nostrils, which he wiped with a finger and rubbed onto his tongue. His eyes had taken on a distant glassy look as if relishing the thought of the pleasure soon to sweep over him.

'*Man of Honour*,' he repeated. 'I enjoyed that one. I still remember the dialogue of that last scene. Won me the FilmLovers Award for Best Actor I recall. And I really could dance then, you know. No doubles or stand-ins.'

He shut his eyes, his entire demeanour softened, relaxed, as the force of the powder got to him.

He pointed to the drinks tray that stood in a corner of the office.

'Pour us a drink. If we are now going to see each other more often, we may as well get to know each other.'

I poured us both a drink, gleefully anticipating the camaraderie and discourse to come. An exchange of backstories, anecdotes shared, details exchanged, all the usual building blocks that turn acquaintanceships into friendships.

But it was not to be.

For two hours, we sat there, across his table, drinks in hand while he, the self-absorbed old egomaniac, talked exclusively about himself.

He, India's greatest star, was now India's greatest producer!

I knew this was not true, as I had not yet seen a single movie with him credited as producer.

He was still all powerful in Bollywood, a man who could make or break careers!

I seriously doubted this. Bollywood tolerates no weakness or infirmity. This tired old addict would command little respect in a business obsessed by looks and vigour.

And he could sleep with any starlet or star he chose; such was his lasting charm and virility!

Impossible. Given what was going up his nose, I was pretty sure that it was more than just his eyelids that drooped.

I found myself in a difficult position.

I had really wanted to like this man, this great icon of a bygone era.

I wanted to be his friend and tell others about the wonderful times we shared together.

But I could not.

Unlike the humble, loveable, honourable characters he portrayed on screen, in life he was an obnoxious, arrogant, self-absorbed prat.

And he was rude to his daughter.

But business is business.

'Tell me about your friendship with Avzal Bhai,' I asked.

'We grew up in the same building, went to the same school. We were inseparable. Two boys with big dreams and no means to make them possible. He always looked after me. I was a Hindu living in a Muslim neighbourhood. He was my friend, my protector.

Eventually, I was "discovered" while acting in a college drama competition. He was "discovered" when he took bets on who would win the competition and the impressive manner in which he persuaded the judges to vote his way.

I went into the movies. He went into the organisation. But we always stayed in touch. Shared a meal now and then, called each other from time to time.

I attended his wedding, he attended mine. He understood that our meetings had to be low-key, discreet. In those days, actors were not supposed to hobnob with people in his field of business, and the people in his business would never trust an actor.'

By now, the alcohol and the drugs were starting to erase his inhibitions.

'Not like today where organisations like yours are our biggest financiers. They send us their black money, and we turn it into legitimate box-office gains. Everyone wants to be a producer.

Pigs! All cash and no class!'

And so on it went.

Every two or three days I rang the bell on the door with the flashing red light (permanently un-fixed), was led by his silent, hostile daughter to his office and spent the best part of the evening pouring him drinks and listening to his boastful ramblings about his talent, his successes, his prowess and his powers.

It was four or five hours of sheer boredom, but it was my job.

I tried hard, but found no reason to warm to him.

When people came to his office to talk to him about production matters, he shouted at them.

When the director of his movie approached him for clarification on some matter or the other, he was insufferably rude.

When his leading man, Akhtar Khan, dropped by for a cup of tea and a chat, Bunty listened carefully, ignored the question he was being asked and instead, gave him some unsolicited advice on the art of acting.

Once he had left Bunty unloaded.

'That third-rate ham, that inept, bumbling ten-take incompetent!

As much emotion as an iceberg!

He's not an actor,' Bunty roared at me, 'he's a third-rate performer.

What's more, he is so stupid, he does not even know the difference.

Actors today! All muscle and shaven chests!

In my day, it did not matter that leading men were a little chubby or had double chins or receding hairlines.

All that mattered was that they had talent. They could bring tears to the eye of a stone statue. They knew pathos. They knew emotion.

Today all they know about acting is when to take their shirts off!'

Explosions of derision and self-pity were common with him. And I was merely his sounding board.

The last audience he had left.

I realised our relationship would always be one of master and servant, never destined to develop into the familiarity I had hoped for.

But I was wrong.

One evening, some 18 months after I had started delivering Bunty Bhaskar his parcels, things changed dramatically.

I took him his parcel around 7 p.m. and found him in a particularly morose frame of mind.

'Sit with me, Ricki,' he pleaded. 'Don't leave me here to spend another evening alone.'

That night, I genuinely had other plans. Rashid and the boys were taking me out to help celebrate my 26th birthday.

'Bunty sir,' I replied, 'I cannot stay tonight. It is my birthday, and I was going...'

'Birthday? Then we have to celebrate. No! I will not take no for an answer.'

He immediately helped himself to the parcel I had brought him and within a few minutes, euphoria had set in and he was on top of the world.

'Come on, Ricki, tonight we hit the town. I will teach you how to celebrate,' he yelled as he tossed me his car keys. 'I know a bar that you will like.'

What could I do?

Offend him and by so doing, anger Avzal Bhai?

And anyway, how bad could it be? The old boy was already so high, he'd be asleep in an hour or two. I could then take him home and still have time to catch up with the birthday party.

'Alright, Bunty sir,' I replied, 'you are very kind. I can't drive cars, but if you are willing to trust me, I will drive you there in a far more enjoyable way.'

Bunty loved Saraswati.

'Faster, Ricki, faster,' he kept shouting.

He hung out the side, singing a song from one of his great hits, a song that, in the movie, he sang while riding a motorcycle.

Thankfully, it was dark enough for people not to recognise the madman laughing and singing out loud, shouting at passing motorists and behaving like an excited child.

'I feel young again, Ricki,' he shouted at me over the sound of Saraswati's rumbling exhaust.

'My God, how I've missed this. The wind, the noise, the smell. From now on, wherever we go, we go in your rickshaw!'

Walking into bars and restaurants with Bunty Bhaskar gave me my first insight into what real fame must feel like.

When he entered a room, the babble of the assembled crowd would cease immediately as people caught sight of him and stared in disbelief.

Then a low mumble of exclamations would start around the room.

'My God...look.'

'Is that Bunty Bhaskar?'

'I can't believe my eyes.'

'In the flesh.'

'Who would have thought'...and so on it went.

Disbelief was then followed quickly by a desire to get as close to the great man as possible.

I am told that in the West, when you see a celebrity, it is considered bad manners to stare or to approach them.

In India it is considered rude to look the other way.

Perhaps the difference is that in the West, fame is an embarrassment.

In India, fame is an achievement. People work hard to achieve it, so why not acknowledge it?

Greatness is something to be gawped at, and then, it is something to be grasped at.

As he walked from the door into the room, people would get up to shake his hands, touch his feet to ask his blessings, thrust mobile cameras in his face and ask for selfies with him.

In seconds, he would be swamped by adoring fans.

And Bunty loved it.

I once actually saw him shaking hands with one fan, talking to a second, raising his head to pose for a third and all the while, signing an autograph for the fourth.

Really, no one could multi-bask like Bunty Bhaskar.

I soon also realised that he had a bar behaviour that never changed.

He would immediately order a bottle of whisky. Foreign of course.

'Indian whisky tastes perfectly good, Ricki,' he once confided in me, 'but it doesn't play well with the public. "What a cheap bastard," they would say.'

He would, with three of four large drinks, finish half the bottle; then, bottle in hand, he would work the room. From table to table, greeting people, humbly voicing his gratitude for the platitudes they heaped on him and filling their glasses with whisky.

'Please, my friend, join me in a drink,' he'd say.

Whether they were drinking gin, rum, vodka, a Martini or Manhattan, he'd pour a peg of his whisky into their glass.

It is a testimony to his star power, that even now years past his heyday, all the times I saw him do that, no one ever objected or punched his lights out.

Having a drink ruined was well worth the status gained of being able to tell people, 'Last night I had a drink with my friend Bunty Bhaskar.'

That particular night, we visited four bars in quick succession.

By the end of the bottle at the fourth establishment, Bunty was well away, wrapped in the arms of alcohol, getting loud and fractious.

I deemed it best we leave. I sent Rashid a text telling him I would soon be with them.

Together we walked out onto the street where I tried to steer my weaving, stumbling charge towards where Saraswati was parked.

As we staggered along, I saw two young men approach from the other side of the road. From the way they too were weaving across the pavement, I quickly realised that they were as drunk as Bunty was.

As they passed us, they recognized him.

'Hey, that is...eh...that's...what's his name?' said one.

'Yeah...what's his name! Big star, my mother's favourite,' said his companion.

Before I could get Bunty away, one had pulled out his camera and the other, no doubt hoping to impress his mother, threw an arm around Bunty's neck, trying to get close for the photo his friend was about to take.

Bunty roared in anger, pushing the man back and squaring up to his companion, a lion about to charge.

'Sons of whores! Gutter filth! No-class cretins! You have the manners of a Pakistani,' he spat at them in disgust.

The two men stopped smiling. I could see that the insult had struck home.

The Indian male is, by and large, a placid beast. Most epithets he will accept good naturedly, with a wobble of the head and a smile on his face.

But you cannot call him a Pakistani.

That is a blow too low.

The men bristled and took a step forward threateningly.

It was time to step in.

'Gentlemen, please, you are interrupting one of India's greatest actors from preparing for his next role.'

They stopped, confused.

I continued before they could say anything.

'In his next role, Mr Bhaskar is playing a wealthy industrialist who loses his entire family when their private yacht sinks in the Andaman Sea.

In grief, he loses his mind and his fight with alcohol. Alone and drunk, he wanders the streets at night, ranting at the world and slipping into insanity.'

The men stood back, staring at Bunty intently.

'Gentlemen, you are watching a master crafting his performance.

To find the right inspiration, the right colour, Mr Bhaskar goes around the bars to drink what he believes his character would drink. He watches the drunks there and then tries out various techniques that he hopes will allow a teetotaller like him to successfully affect the behaviour of a drunk. Please stand back and watch, but please, do not interrupt his flow.'

As if on cue, Bunty let loose with another round of invectives, even more loudly and forcefully than the first.

'You mean he actually gets drunk just to see what it feels like, then walks about shouting and swearing?' asked one of the men.

'That must be what they call Method School,' the other opined knowingly.

I could not bring myself to tell them that Bunty's school of acting was more Scotch and soda than Stanislavski.

They immediately reverted to the reflex action of all Indians who believe they may be about to witness a film being shot on the street.

They moved in closer and turned into film critics.

Bunty was now weaving round in circles, screaming at the world and trying to pull a road sign out of the pavement, no doubt to attack the men with.

'What creativity,' said one man, wobbling his head in approval.

'Yes, yes…he feels; therefore he is!' the Method School devotee nodded knowingly.

At this moment, I noticed Bunty was turning puce. Then, as the bile in his throat met the booze in his stomach, the great genius belched, bent over and threw up all over the men's shoes.

They were almost speechless.

'Wa, wa…what artistry,' said the first in awe.

'It feels so…real,' gulped his friend, wriggling his toes as colourful chunks of Bunty's artistry seeped into his open-toed sandals.

Spontaneously, they applauded.

What is it with actors?

They may be limp, wasted, asleep, even comatose, but the slightest hint of applause and they revive like water revives a wilting plant.

On autopilot, Bunty immediately straightened up, wiped his mouth and began to launch into an acceptance speech.

I grabbed him by the arms, pushed him along to where we had left Saraswati and bundled him in.

Fortunately, he immediately fell asleep and I could safely drive him home.

The house was entirely dark when we got there.

I dragged Bunty up the front stairs and rang the bell.

Bunty, head on my shoulder, had now awoken and was singing a selection of great love songs of the 60's.

Eventually lights went on, and I heard the door latch pulled open.

Kalpana, obviously awoken from her sleep, stood there, arms folded across her chest, eyes ablaze.

'You drunken old fool,' she said to Bunty, 'be quiet and get to bed. Get to bed now!'

Bunty, chastened but not completely cowed, staggered in, pinching her on the behind as he walked past her. She jumped and turned on me in fury.

'This is what you do to him? Drag him to disreputable places and let him get drunk? Don't you ever lead him astray again!'

With that she slammed the door in my face and the light over the porch went out.

I stood there in darkness, not at all put out by the injustice of her accusation or the ferocity of her tone.

None of that entered my head.

Instead, my vision went woozy and my heart started beating at the speed of a *tabla* being played by four hands.

I had just seen Kalpana in a short, hip-length nightshirt with a skimpy shawl wrapped around her shoulders.

Her hair, usually worn over her head in a severe bun, fell loose around her shoulders, tousled and mussed, framing her face and softening her features.

Her eyes, without her heavy black-framed glasses around them, looked large and full of fire, flashing like two black sapphires.

Her legs looked long and lean.

Her arms strong and smooth.

The curve of her backside, pushing against the thin fabric of her nightshirt looked every bit as perfectly rounded as a ripe alphonso.

I drove home that night lost in a trance.

I had visions of her and me, dancing around a rickshaw parked on a moonlit beach. Fully clothed (thinking of the censors even in my fantasies) we would enter the ocean, rolling around in the surf. We would serenade each other with vows of eternal love until finally, as the song ended, she would cling to me with ill-concealed passion.

I even had a little ditty running around in my head with the subtitles required for foreign release.

Kalpana, oh Kalpana
Kab hogi tu apana? (When will you be mine?)
De na mujhe tera pyaar. (Give me your love)
Kalpana, oh Kalpana,
Dekha mene sapana, (I have seen a dream)
Jsme tu hai meri superstar. (In which you are my superstar)

OK, not quite a Salim-Javed Top Ten but quite marketable, I thought.

No doubt about it, I had the 'so-that's-what's-under-a-sari' shakes.

You see, growing up, most of us Indian village boys only see our womenfolk clad in saris. Graceful garment of course, but worn the traditional way it covers every inch of the wearer from shoulders down to ankles, revealing nothing.

Of course we know our women have thighs and hips and cheeks on their backsides.

But until we actually manage to get a glimpse of what lies under a sari, as I just had, we never fully understand the glory of creation or its disruptive potential.

I never made it to the party that night.

I wanted to be alone with my fantasies.

I returned to my little apartment behind the office and stretched out on my bed.

Sleep was impossible. Every way I turned, my ardour seemed to get in the way of my comfort.

All I could think about were those gentle, inviting curves covered in smooth, milk chocolate.

Cadbury's would never satisfy again.

At 6 that morning, I was still tossing and turning and thinking of her, when my phone rang.

It was Bunty.

'My hero, my saviour,' he shouted.

'No sir, I just…'

'Magnificent! Selfless! Noble warrior! The way you handled those six thugs!'

'Actually just two, sir. I….'

'The way you held them back, then despatched them so I could make a dignified exit!'

Clearly drink had wiped most of his memory.

'Well, not really, sir. I just…'

He would not be stopped.

'Your courage must be repaid. You deserve to be showered in gold.'

OK, this I could listen to.

'I have the perfect reward. You will now work for me. Personal Assistant to Bunty Bhaskar! From now on, wherever I go, you go!'

My heart sank. The thought of spending my life around that drunk, drugged-up egomaniac deflated all passion in an instant.

'No, no sir,' I stammered, 'I have a job. Remember, sir, I work for your friend Avzal.'

'No problem,' he shouted back at me. 'I will speak to Avzal. He will deny me nothing. Be at the studio at 3 p.m. today, and we will work out the details.'

With that, he was gone.

Sure enough, at 10 that morning, Imtiaz's ancient Padmini drove into the office compound, and a grinning Avzal emerged.

He sat across from me in the office, chuckling to himself.

'So, you really have impressed Mr Bhaskar,' he started.

'Only doing what you asked, Boss. Just looking after your friend.'

'Still, I never thought you had it in you to fight off 10 men.'

It was growing with every telling.

'Oh no, sir,' I blushed, 'Mr Bhaskar gets confused. It was only seven.'

Well, it never hurts to give the boss something to remember at bonus time.

'He wants you to work for him full time.'

I jumped in quickly.

'No, sir, I told him that was not possible. I work for you.'

He nodded. 'Yes, but I think this may not be such a bad idea. Right now, you deliver to him then you leave. But as his PA you would be there all day long. You will get to know everyone there much quicker. And being his PA, they are far more likely to trust you. There is a huge business opportunity there, Ricki. This will give you the opportunity to really exploit it.'

I knew there was no arguing with him.

He misread the disappointment showing on my face.

'Don't worry,' he consoled me, 'you will still also continue to work for me. You can continue to look after the rickshaws here, look after your old clients, make a few deliveries. Cheer up, Ricki. You will always work for me! Look at this as a small promotion. Make it work, grow the business and you will do very well out of it.'

Sure enough, that afternoon, I was appointed Bunty Bhaskar's Personal Assistant. Unpaid!

The tight bastard.

Kalpana simply glowered in the corner as Bunty summoned together all the crew and cast working on the studio floor and made a grandiose speech about how, accosted by twenty thugs, he and I fought them off together, like Batman and Robin. He at the forefront of the battle repulsing attack after attack. Me at the rear watching his back.

In one afternoon, I had gone from the Lone Avenger to Wimpy sidekick.

Such was life with Bunty Bhaskar.

His changes of mood, his sudden turns from kindly uncle to loudmouth to lunatic perplexed me.

He could, depending on his mood, be either ill-mannered nouveau riche or high-minded old school.

One of his favourite hobby horses was the difference between the old India and the new mood of the nation.

He often lamented the loss of the old ways; a gentler, easier time before the Indian economic boom made money and material success the focus of all achievement.

One afternoon he insisted we take tea at his club. We sat on the large verandah, while waiters scurried about us, ignoring other members for the privilege of serving the wonderful Mr Bhaskar.

Bunty was grace itself, waving at fellow members, smiling at one and all, chatting to passers-by.

The verandah overlooks the club's cricket pitch; a match between his club and their opposition from down the road was taking place.

Good-naturedly, Bunty watched as the batsmen ran and fieldsmen hurled themselves across the turf.

For those reading this who may not be familiar with cricket, Americans or Martians say, let me just tell you that cricket is a sport that the British invented, the Indians perfected and the Australians turned into open warfare.

Unfortunately, the match in front of us was not being played in the time-honoured traditions of Indian cricket; graciously and genially.

It was more Aussie gamesmanship than Indian sportsmanship.

The wicketkeeper was obviously haranguing the batsman; the bowler was scowling at the umpire; the fieldsmen were trying to upset the batting pair; words were being exchanged.

Bunty's mood changed from avuncular to aggravated.

He eyed the on-field activities silently but was obviously fuming inside. Silently, he took it all in; the lip from slip, the insults from infield, players having a bitch on the pitch.

Suddenly, the bowler appealed for an LBW (Love Beats Walls, for you Americans), which the umpire turned down.

The bowler turned on the umpire and even to us sitting at a distance, most of his anger was audible.

The words 'blind' and 'bribed' and 'buffoon' floated across the boundary towards us.

Suddenly, Bunty could take no more.

With a voice that in turn was loud enough to carry to the wicket, he was off.

'Look! Look!' he screamed to all about him. 'This is the problem with this country today. This is what will ruin us.

Win, win, win. Do anything to win!

Win every time, all the time.

Everyone always pushing, fighting, clawing to win at everything.

How is that possible?

Have we forgotten that for every winner there has to be a loser?

Our culture teaches us to recognise that. Our faith teaches us to accept that.'

I tried to pull him back down, but the actor had found his audience.

'Have we forgotten the one quality that made India famous?

We lost brilliantly!

With a smile! With conviction!!

Since Independence, we have been the world's most like-able losers.

We lost at cricket, we lost at hockey, we lost out in the partition, we lost out with Tibet, we lost out as a global force, we lost out on the Security Council, we even lose at chess and we invented the bloody thing!

But, so what?

We learnt to lose so well, we won respect.

Look at us now,' he screamed loudly enough for the lady at the next table to drop her fruit cake into her tea cup, 'aggression, insults, bad behaviour.

We treat each other with no respect, no kindness.

We are the nation that gave the world non-violence, tolerance, yoga.

We had the highest spiritual values.

We knew this life was a test, not the prize.

But now we scream at each other; we stab each other in the back; we climb over each other; we argue with the umpire.

Why? Why?

I will tell you why!

Because we want to be like everyone else.

We want to be as aggressive as the Australians, as ruthless as the Russians, as ambitious as the Americans, as cold-hearted as the Germans, as cut-throat as the Chinese, as arrogant as the British.

We want to send machines to Mars when we can't even send all our children to school!

We want technology for all when most don't even have toilets!

We want to be anyone we can.

We just don't want to be ourselves, Indian!

Where are the simple, forgiving, friendly, kind people I grew up with?

Where have all the real Indians gone?'

I could have told him. Canada! That other great nation that wins at nothing.

I hoped with this final show of despair he had exhausted his diatribe, but Bunty Bhaskar had not finished. He pointed at one of the fieldsmen who had stopped and moved closer towards us to watch the Bunty Show.

'Look at that filthy fellow,' he said pointing at the poor man's grass-stained trousers.

'Slithering and sliding on the field like urchins playing in the mud.

If a ball is destined for the boundary, so be it. No dive can alter its destiny.

They are like low-life lizards, wriggling around on their stomachs.

In my day, a fieldsman always stood proud on his feet, tall and upright as a real man should.

We may have lost every match we played.

But we never lost our dignity!'

With that final fulmination, having sufficiently vented his spleen, Bunty Bhaskar drew himself to his full height, turned around and, chin held high, marched towards the exit.

Everyone stared as he swept along the verandah; all the other members, the waiters, the 13 men on the field and both umpires, all speechless, mouths agape.

Bunty Bhaskar stopped the game that colonial subjugation, two World Wars, one bloody Partition, three border skirmishes, communal riots, famine, flood and terrorist attacks could not stop.

It was a power-plus performance.

I have to admit though, for all his faults, he could also be a generous friend.

I quickly realised that his club would be an ideal location to expand our business.

A place where exhausted businessmen went to relax and housewives went to dispel their boredom.

Where gambling debts mounted up at card and billiard tables, where the bar tabs could swell alarmingly.

In our business, plenty of stress means plenty of scope.

'Does Avzal Bhai know about your club, sir?' I asked innocently one day. 'I think he would like it. It would really help his business, sir, getting to know all those important people.'

Bunty was intrigued. 'You think he could profit from those poseurs? They certainly have the money to avail themselves of Avzal's product line-up. I will speak to Avzal about it. If it helps him, I'm all for it.'

A few days later he called me up to the office. I was down on the studio floor, talking to the crew, learning about the movie business.

'Avzal really like your idea about the club. But he does not want his name associated with it or to make himself that conspicuous. He suggests I nominate you to become a member, and you can then service the members there as you service me.'

Within days he had me proposed, found someone I have never met to provide a flawless character reference and within a few months, I was a member of the club, enjoying tea and fruit cake with Mumbai's richest and finest.

With one stroke of Bunty's largesse I went from penniless parasite to prosperous player.

That was the man.

Hard to like. And harder to comprehend.

12

ADD THE ROMANCE

If you have ever wondered what a PA does, I can tell you.

Everything!

I drove him around, fetched and carried, made his tea, poured his drinks, cleaned him up when drunk, took him home when high, pulled him out of fights, delivered his laundry, cleaned up his office and when needed, wiped his nose.

As jobs go, it was hell.

But I have to admit that it did have its compensations.

From the window of his office, I got to watch his movie being shot.

I loved that. Particularly the dance sequence with 20 attractive women jiggling about.

I met writers, actors, lighting men, sound recordists, directors, cameramen, electricians, all the cast and crew involved in Bunty's movie *When the Heart Breaks*.

I picked their brains, asked about their jobs, listened to their ideas and chummed up to one and all.

Everyone we met Bunty introduced me as Ricki, the PA who could get anything, anytime.

At first, people were suspicious and kept their distance.

But in the end, desire always wins out over discretion, and I started to add to our list of clients.

A nervous assistant director here, an anxious set decorator there.

Ageing dancers desperate for a final shot of youthful vitality were an easy mark.

Inexperienced camera boys, runners and production assistants used me to add edge to their energy.

Experienced choreographers, lighting directors and cameramen used me to take the edge off their insecurities.

Grips and gaffers, worried about the next job, the next paycheck, used me to ward off their anxieties.

Junior artists, nervous about performing with stars, used me to obtain a shot of courage.

To everyone I was Ricki the provider.

Their friend the candyman. On call, whenever needed.

Ignored during the day and on speed dial at night.

As word spread, I started getting calls from the other studios on the lot.

At Studio 3, where Urmila Gatonde and Yasin Khan were shooting a college romcom called *Innocent Hearts*, Urmila called on me to help her lose the 15 years that had passed since she was last at college, and Yasin used me to ease the pain of the corset that trimmed him down to a youthful 42-inch waist (old-fashioned Indian trim).

At Studio 9, where writer, director and star Ibrahim Khan was making another of his ultra-nationalistic melodramas, this one entitled *My Land, My Blood*, 200 extras dressed as Indian and Chinese soldiers relied on me to ease the boredom of days spent waiting for Mr Khan to sober up long enough to actually shoot something.

The secret to our business success at the studio was best explained to me one evening by an exhausted old comic named Ekchimchi Khan. 'This is not about trying to find pleasure, Ricki,' he moaned as he paid for his delivery. 'It's about trying to find inspiration.'

Within two years, business from Glorious Cine Studios exceeded all our earlier expectations.

Obviously, Avzal Bhai was delighted.

'You have turned this into one of our biggest profit centres, Ricki.

Wah, wah.'

He turned to Imtiaz sitting beside him. 'Did I not tell you this was a good plan?' Imtiaz simply scowled.

Avzal Bhai thumped him on the back and laughed.

'He is upset because now that you look after the studio, he does not get to meet his girlfriend there as often as he did. Never mind, old friend. You are a fighter, not a lover.'

This was news to me.

Imtiaz? He with a face like a constipated rat, with more oil in his hair than the annual output of Bombay High? He had a girlfriend?

Really, I had to start putting myself out there more.

But who could find the time?

Bunty Bhaskar was a 24-hour responsibility.

When he was too drugged up to walk, I drove him home.

When Kalpana locked him out of the house for his drunk and disorderly behaviour, I found him a hotel room for the night.

When he got into fights, which happened often, I got him out of them.

When his creditors came calling, I arranged for Avzal Bhai to get them off his back.

And saddest of all, when he spent lonely drunken nights in his office, tearfully raging at the world around him, I sat with him, listening to his threats and taking his abuse.

For me, this was the job from hell, being party to the dissolution and destruction of someone who had once been an idol of mine, mean old bastard that he was.

But it had one major compensation.

I got to spend more time in Kalpana's company.

At first, she wanted to have nothing to do with me. But as time passed, she would agree to share an *idli sambar*[9] in the studio canteen with me.

Being the boss's daughter, the others took orders from her, listened to her, were polite to her, but no one made friends with her.

How could they be sure that a complaint or gripe would not make it back to Bunty's ear?

---

9 Rice cakes and spicy curry. Pride of the South.

Her loneliness, coupled with the fact that every time she looked round, she saw me hanging about somewhere, gradually led to a softening of her attitude towards me.

She made it very clear from the outset that she could never really be friends with someone in my line of work.

'You are a leech, feeding off the misery of others,' she once told me.

I wobbled my head with what I hope was a chastened look on my face.

'You are a crook, a thief. You will go to jail one day.'

Despite the glaring error in my job description, I wobbled harder in mute agreement.

'I could never have feelings for anyone who worked for the people you work for.'

I changed from a wobble to a head shake as if acknowledging the hideous nature of the people I worked with.

But I felt a definite spark of hope.

I had never mentioned the possibility of us having feelings for each other.

Her mentioning it had to be a good sign, right?

Most evenings, after I had made my deliveries around the various studio lots and sound stages, Kalpana and I would sit in the canteen, two chais and an *idli sambar* between us, growing closer with each admonition and disparaging comment she dished out.

She told me a little about herself.

She was an only child.

She blamed her father for her lonely, unhappy childhood, trapped in a big house with no friends.

She blamed her father for her mother's mental decline and eventual death.

She blamed her father for having to give up her job as teacher at a local state school (maths and chemistry) and having to look after him.

She hated being a production assistant, the movie business, spending time on sets, acting like a secretary, having to take finance men on tours of the studio, and of course, she blamed her father for this.

What a wonderful woman, I thought.

Devoted to someone she detests.

Surely that augured well for me?

One evening, when I went up the stairs to Bunty's office, I found him in a particularly agitated state.

He was sprawled on his couch, telltale white powder on his shirt front and face.

Papers lay strewn around the office, drawers pulled out, the chair at his desk upended.

I had seen this before. The aftermath of a particularly stormy investor meeting.

'Fools. Philistines. Pharasees,' he screamed. 'Make it fast. Make it cheap. Make it big. Just because they have the money, they think they have the right to come here and shout at me?

They know nothing. Where is the art? Where is the imagination? Where is the idea?

They fill my safe with their filthy black money, and suddenly they think they can tell me how to make a blockbuster hit.'

I turned to look at the safe and continued to stare at it in complete disbelief.

The old fool had left the doors wide open and there it stood, some seven feet tall, four feet wide, four feet deep and completely filled, top to bottom, with banknotes. Stacks and stacks of them, crammed in haphazardly, filling the safe and some spilling out onto the floor below.

He saw me looking at it.

'Yes, that. They bring me their crores of cash when their mattresses are bursting and there is no more space under their floorboards.

They have nowhere else to put it, so they leave it here and want an instant hit in return.

Every time there is a government crackdown on black money, they turn into "creative consultants".

Why is it that the moment you call someone a client, they suddenly think they have talent?'

At this moment, the office door flew open and Kalpana walked in.

'Is it not time we headed home,' she started to say, then stopped in her tracks, taking in the scene before her.

Clearly, the sight of the open safe came as a shock to her too.

'Father,' she screamed, 'this is not our money! It belongs to others who have trusted you with it!'

Then, noticing me standing there, 'How can you leave it open and unlocked like that for...for...just anyone to see?'

Her father waved a hand at her.

'Stop nagging, girl. Ricki is Avzal's man. That means he is 100% trustworthy. Otherwise, Avzal would have had him turned into mini *kebabs* for his *kutta* by now.'

OK! Finally I decided I had had enough!

You will recall over the course of this journey of mine, I have been called several rather unsavoury names by the people I have dealt with.

Frog, pariah, urchin, cockroach, stupid, runt and chintu, even though I stand a proud and perfectly proportioned five feet seven inches tall.

But *kebabs* for Avzal's dogs?

This was too much for a man a full two inches taller than the national average to take silently.

I decided it was time to add some inches to my pride.

'Kalpana madam, you may not be aware, but I am the one who looks after your father when you storm out of the studio in a huff every evening.

I help change his clothes when he throws up over them.

I drive him around when he is too drunk to do so safely.

I even find and return his wallet, his car keys, even the keys to your house when he leaves them behind in the bars I accompany him to.

All this I do when you have given up on him and gone home.

If I had wanted to take advantage of him, or you, I have had a dozen chances or more to do so.

Perhaps madam, you may want to judge me for who I am rather than what you think I do.

I give people what they want…no more no less.

Like the *cigarettewalla* on every street corner, the *paanwalla* next to him, the liquor mart down the street. What they sell may not meet your high standards, madam, but for millions of Indians these are the only comforts, few moments of joy they have in their harsh, miserable lives.

What I do helps them deal with the ugliness of their present, and yes, it helps me cater for my future.

No rich father for me to rail against, madam.

No easy life with three meals provided.

You think that because of what I do I am beneath you, not worthy of your friendship or trust.

Well, madam, let me tell you this.

In my business, you don't survive unless you are scrupulously honest. 100% trustworthy!

My bosses don't believe in second chances.

In your business, you get it wrong and you just shoot it again. But in my business, madam, if we get it wrong we just get shot. There are no retakes because there can be no mistakes.'

I stopped there, taken aback by this terrible bit of word play that had popped out of my mouth.

Up to that point, I was impressing myself beyond words.

Perhaps the hobnobbing I had been doing with writers and script editors, reading all those foreign authors was paying off?

But the last line was truly a bomb. Pure Avzal Bhai!

I really would have to look for another job before too much longer.

Bunty Bhaskar of course loved it. He clapped with glee.

'Oh what dialogue. What a comeback. You did not expect that, did you my darling daughter? Ricki, you should be writing scripts.

I know! You are now my new script advisor. You will read all the scripts I get sent!'

Kalpana, much to my surprise, looked sheepish.

She gazed down at her feet.

'I am sorry if I seem unfriendly. I truly hate what you do. But yes, I have seen how you care for my father, and I think, deep inside, you are a good man. I am willing to take that into consideration.'

This I looked upon gratefully. This new role suited me fine.

I can do 'good boy gone wrong' as well as any actor. I've seen it a hundred times. It's probably the second-most common Bollywood theme after 'rich father accepts pauper as son-in-law after said pauper saves rich man's favourite daughter from burning car wreck'.

The tension of the scene, though, was considerably ruined by the loud snores emanating from the region of the couch.

Bunty Bhaskar, in the best traditions of the Indian movie-goer, had got bored by the lack of action during the 'talk-talk' bits and had fallen asleep.

'I am sorry if I seem unkind, Ricki. Please, no more madam. Call me Kalpana.'

It was time to show her just how big a man the runt really was.

'Consider it forgotten, Kalpana. Now, let's get this sorted out. You put all the money back in the safe. Lock it up well. I will clean up the mess here and get your father sobered up enough to get him down the stairs and into my rickshaw. Then, I will drive you both home.'

She nodded silently. Then she walked up to me, looked straight into my eyes, and simply whispered a tiny 'thank you'.

I saw the change in her expression towards me.

Definitely a little less *Rickshawalla* and…perhaps…a bit more Romeo?

SECOND INTERMISSION

13

CUE THE STORM ON THE HORIZON

Gradually, my relationship with Kalpana took a friendlier turn.

Rather than scowl when she saw me, she would give me a small smile.

Rather than berate me for delivering those packages to her father, she would sigh tolerantly.

She would allow me to take her home in Saraswati and even waved goodbye when I left her there.

One day, on the way home, I asked if she would like a cup of coffee.

She accepted.

We stopped at a small cafe next to St Andrew's Church. The cup of coffee lasted a good two hours as we talked about her life, my life and everything in between.

Eventually, the coffee stops turned into walks along the Carter Road seafront. (Yes, that very same place. Only now, I was on the other side of the rocks).

We shared *sitaphal*[10] ice creams and *pani puris*[11] and, over the course of the next six months, all our secrets.

I told her about my humble position in life, my village background, my start as a rickshaw driver, my earnest belief in the importance of seizing an opportunity first, considering its ramifications later.

She just smiled and shrugged.

'A man is good or bad whatever the situation of his birth,' she said.

They must train teachers in this sort of 'Nation of Equals' nonsense.

I told her my real name. She thought about it for a moment then told me that to her, I would always be Ricki.

That's it! Ricki I am forever!

We watched movies together when I even confessed my deep and undying love for Deepika.

She took it all with grace and good humour.

But the biggest change of all was the change she made to my wardrobe.

---

10 The Hindi word for a Custard Apple, the fruit with so many seeds, it involves more spitting than swallowing.

11 Yet more street food stuff. After all, you can't sit through a 18 reel marathon without something to snack on.

As a production assistant, she often helped the wardrobe department with finding new looks, new designs, and new styles of clothing.

She soon took to restyling me.

At Kalpana's insistence, my beloved Indian safari suits, despite their extra-wide lapels and mock ivory buttons, were bundled up and thrown into the incinerator at the studio lot.

'No class,' she said shaking her head at me.

'You have the money, Ricki. The only way newly rich people can pretend to have taste is by buying expensive labels.'

With her help, I now dressed in English sports coats, German shirts, French ties, American jeans, Japanese T-shirts with senseless words on them and Italian leather shoes.

I went from Indian comfortable to foreign fop in the wink of an eye.

Our shopping trips would last all Saturday long, ending up at one of the restaurants in the large malls we frequented.

Despite the comfort and closeness in our relationship, I knew my job would always be a barrier between us.

She made it clear that no matter what she felt for me, until I gave up my current life, we had little future together.

How could I explain to her that giving up my current life would probably result in me giving up life itself?

That little impediment apart, all was running smoothly with the 'boy meets girl' subplot.

The business side of things, though, had started to take an alarming turn.

As I have said, our sales were growing rapidly.

The three additional rickshaws gave us a great deal of extra capacity, and the success we enjoyed at the studio was growing exponentially.

No surprise then that it all came to the attention of Salgaonkar's client service team that someone was taking clients away from them, right under their very noses.

The beginning of the end was brought to my notice by Salim, my chemist friend and customer.

'Ricki,' he confessed one day when I went to drop off his latest order, 'I have a problem. Yesterday I got a visit from this man.'

He held out a business card for me to look at. It read:

Shri Nandu Talpade.
Area Coordinator.
Govind Industries.

Govind was Salgaonkar's younger brother, and Govind Industries was a well-known shell for their smuggling and drug-running business.

The opposition was onto us.

Clearly, Salim was shaken.

'He brought three of his associates with him, and they threatened to burn down my store and hurt my parents if I did not start buying from them. I'm sorry, Ricki, but they asked me who I was dealing with, who was organising your operation, and I gave them your name. They were quite insistent.'

Salim was not a brave man, and I felt no ill will at his having dropped me in it.

After all, this was our fight, not his fight.

'Look,' he said, 'they even left me with a small sample of their product as a sign of their good faith. They said they would be back in a week to take my first order.'

I looked at the small package in his hands. It was a bright-yellow box, the sort that Indian sweets are sold in, and on top were printed the words 'Compliments of Govind Industries'.

Clearly they felt they had nothing to fear from a little publicity.

My mind focussed on the time frame involved.

A week.

After years of establishing a business; building up a client base; forming a network of allies, emissaries, contacts and confidants, it could all end in a week.

I had no doubt that Salim would only be the first. One by one they would approach all our clients, squeezing us out of the business through the sheer ferocity of their anger.

Hell hath no fury like a smuggler scorned.

I must tell you that for the very first time since I embarked on this road, since the night I first met Avzal Bhai and all that followed, I was genuinely scared.

When organisations such as ours clash, no mercy is shown. There would be blood spilled, savagery unleashed on operatives from both sides.

And little old Ricki Shah, lead man of the Bade Mian operation in the heart of Salgaonkar territory, would be the first to face the fire.

I tried to keep my voice as controlled as possible.

'Salim my friend,' I said, smiling brightly, 'have no fear. This will be resolved within a week. No one will touch you, and we will go back to doing things the way we always have.'

He looked at me uncertainly. Obviously I wasn't doing heartfelt conviction very well.

'Look, as a sign of our good faith, I will take away this measly free sample he left you and, instead, give you one of our larger family-fun-sized packages at absolutely no cost. You sell it on as usual, make your profit and leave everything else to us.'

With that, and refusing the customary cup of tea I shared with him on visits, I left.

I rang Avzal Bhai on my way, and he was waiting for me when I got to the office. Imtiaz paced the floor behind him as I told them of my meeting with Salim. He was visibly agitated. The news had already reached them.

'The doctor at Juhu has already rung here in a panic. And the secretary of the Heavenly Delite Apartments in Borivili. And the supermarket at Vile Parle. All with the same story. Salgaonkar's men are threatening them all.'

Avzal sat silently as Imtiaz ranted on about Salgaonkar's ancestry and legitimacy.

Finally, he let out a deep sigh.

'This day was always coming. You cannot put two cockerels in the one henhouse and expect peace. Well, perhaps it's a good thing. Perhaps it's time to settle this once and for all. Time for us to stop sharing Mumbai with that dog and to take it over completely.'

This of course was not what I had wanted to hear.

I'd rather been hoping to be sent on a year-long, all-expenses-paid, fact-finding mission to Phuket or Langkawi.

The cold feeling in my craw was rapidly congealing into an icy mess.

He rose to his feet, picking up the bag he had brought with him.

'I must go talk to Bade Mian and Sheik Mohsin. You two stay here and do nothing. Call in the other rickshaws. Give them the day off. I will be back once the bosses make their decision.'

He reached into the bag and pulled out an old acquaintance.

One I had not seen since that night we scuppered a perfectly good Royal Enfield.

The same blue muzzle. The same wood-grained insets on the handle.

He looked at me.

'If they come for anyone, they'll come for you first, Ricki. Keep this with you always. If any of Salgaonkar's men get here, you have my permission to use it! If they threaten you or any of our clients in your presence, use it!

Then throw it into Bandra Talao. It's completely untraceable, so don't worry.'

'Imtiaz,' he continued, 'keep your blade sharp. It may be needed soon.'

Imtiaz's face broke into the widest smile I have ever seen. Like a veteran extra who knows the one close-up of his entire career is finally at hand.

I, on the other hand, was trying hard to keep my breakfast down.

War was soon to be declared!

And I, a man who survived solely on his wits, was, for the first time, well and truly scared out of them.

14

PLAY FOR THE PATHOS

The Mumbai monsoon, when it hits, washes down like a tidal wave from the heavens, flooding the city and slowing everything that moves to a crawl.

The traffic that night, as I drove Saraswati towards the studio, stood immobile for miles, making passage through our water-logged streets near impossible.

By the time I got to the studio, Bunty Bhaskar's package safely wrapped and dry under the passenger seat in the back, it had gone past 11 p.m.

I had promised Bunty I would have his delivery for him no later than 8 p.m.

I knew he'd be desperate and in a dangerous mood.

With Avzal Bhai's pistol tucked into my belt under my shirt, I walked towards Studio 6, which apart from the still-flashing red light, stood dark and deserted, all work having ceased for the night.

I entered the darkened entranceway, about to head towards the production office where I knew Bunty would be waiting for me impatiently.

I was about to start climbing the stairs, when I was stopped by something I heard.

It was a sound from one of the workrooms that led off the studio floor.

A soft sobbing, someone trying hard to stifle their tears.

I opened the door of what turned out to be the costume department, and there, seated at a table on which lay a collection of clothes, skirts, jackets and shirts, I saw Kalpana, head bent over, cradling her face in her hands.

She was crying softly.

She heard my footsteps and turned towards me.

As the light hit her face, I felt the pit of my stomach drop towards my knees.

Her left eye was almost closed from the bluish bruise that surrounded it.

Her lip was cut, and she was wiping her nose with a blood-spotted piece of cloth.

I tilted her chin towards me and asked as gently as I could, 'Who did this to you?'

'Let it go, Ricki,' she pleaded. 'It's nothing, really.'

I repeated my question.

'Who did this to you?'

I got my answer via a distant scream from the production office above.

'Kalpana, where are you hiding? Bring me my medication. Now damn you. Damn you! Damn you!'

The scream was followed by the sound of a bottle being thrown against a wall.

Bunty was obviously in the depths of an extended withdrawal and out of control.

Denied his nightly comfort, he seemed to have taken leave of his senses, raging, shouting, destroying his office.

A level of desperation only an addict deprived could ever understand.

I turned to walk towards the door, pulling out the pistol as I went.

Kalpana ran after me, caught my hand and cried out to me.

'No, Ricki, please. Listen to me. He doesn't know what he is doing. It's, it's not him. It's a madness he cannot control. Please, listen to me, Ricki, listen to me.'

I stopped and looked at her.

Her face glistened with the tears that ran down her cheeks.

Her hands clutched at mine.

Then, suddenly as if she could take no more, she threw herself against me, clutching me in an embrace and sobbing into my shirt.

Bunty could wait.

Her need was greater.

I sat her down at the central table and sat beside her.

Gently, I wiped her face with a towel lying there.

Gradually the sobbing eased, and she sat there, slumped against me.

I held her until the shivers subsided.

Her suffering was tearing me apart. Rational thought went out of my head.

'Enough is enough, Kalpana.' I said. 'You should not have to live with a monster. I will take care of you. Let's leave all of this and go away tonight. We'll start over in another city. Just the two of us.'

Mushy nonsense of course when I think of it now, but at that moment, I meant every word of it. We would run away; leave all our worries and fears behind; start a new life.

Fortunately, Kalpana is far more sensible than I am.

She smiled and shook her head.

'We cannot, Ricki. Your employers would find us and kill us. They will never let you go. And, I know it sounds silly, but I cannot leave him.'

Above us, it sounded as if Bunty was throwing his office chair against the walls.

'Why?' I asked, 'Why put up with this abuse and mistreatment?'

'I can't leave him, Ricki.'

Then, after a small pause, she added, 'Because he will soon be leaving me.'

My stomach churned. It couldn't be?

In this moment of misery and sorrow, amidst all the pain and unhappiness we were experiencing, could there be a ridiculous Bollywood-esque moment of melodrama descending upon us?

There could!

'It was diagnosed about 2 years ago. A tumour in his brain.'

I could only stare at her in disbelief. She took my hand in hers.

'They say it cannot be operated on. They offered him chemotherapy and radiation, but when he heard that might have caused him to go bald, he refused. He said when he goes, he wants to go out looking like a leading man, not a balding character artist. Bloody actors!

At first, it grew slowly. But now, every day he gets the most excruciating headaches.

The pain drives him mad.

It affects his character, his personality. Haven't you noticed his mood swings?

Night and day. He gets no sleep. He gets no relief.

That's why he relies on you...on your product, so much. He says it's the only thing that helps with the pain.

A few happy minutes when he leaves his body behind and floats away from the suffering he has to live with.

Forgive him his actions, Ricki. Today he got the results of his latest scan.

Not long now, they say.'

I had no words. I was dumbfounded.

This was real life! My life!

How could a scenario so clichéd it had even been abandoned by Bollywood scriptwriters and consigned to the lowest of the low, that disreputable scrap heap of crassness called TV soap opera, intrude into it?

Perhaps life does imitate art? Well, Indian art anyway.

We sat in silence. I held her. She had started crying again. 'What can I do?' I asked. 'What do you want?'

She dried her eyes and shrugged.

'There is not much time left. Please don't think ill of me, Ricki, but I just want it to end. I want him to find peace. To be comfortable.

I want him to see him free from suffering and fear.'

I understood.

Despite all that had happened between them, he was her father and his pain was her pain. She would find no peace until he did.

That night, after I had delivered the package Bunty had been waiting for, after he had taken his dose of relief and fallen into a silent sleep, I sat up with Kalpana. We talked through most of the night.

As midnight fell, we left the studio and walked through the darkened lot, arm in arm, just feeling comforted to be with each other.

Perhaps, knowing the loss that would soon befall her, she was looking for someone to fill that void, someone to lean on.

I was happy to be whoever she wanted me to be.

The showers had stopped, and the night was cool; the scent of the frangipani flowers floated through the clean, rain-washed air.

I thought we were entirely alone until I saw another couple in the distance, seated at a bench, holding onto each other.

It looked as if they too were enjoying the opportunity to be alone.

I pointed to them.

'We are not the only ones sharing the night. They too have found each other.'

Kalpana looked up and then turned me away from the path that would have taken us past the couple, leaving them to their own company.

'Let's not disturb them. It's really sweet how they meet here every single night. Rosie and her man. She works in our make-up department.

He drives here each evening on the dot of 10 p.m. They spend a few hours together and then, at midnight, go their separate ways.

She is a Christian, so her parents would never allow her to go out with a Muslim.

This movie lot, this make-believe land is the one place they can forget the restrictions the world outside puts on them and just celebrate being with each other.'

I smiled. 'He is lucky to be able to share every evening with the woman he loves. He must be a truly faithful man.'

Kalpana looked at me with a quizzical look.

'You should know,' she said. 'That's the man who used to bring father his parcels before you took over. That's Imtiaz.'

15

BUILD TO THE DENOUEMENT

By 4 a.m. that morning, the storm was back with winds that swept through the sleeping city, rattling and shaking the tin roof over my apartment behind the office.

I lay on my bed, unable to find the peace I needed to fall asleep. In fact, I could not even find the courage I needed to shut my eyes for fear of Salgaonkar's men breaking through the door and tearing me to pieces.

The TV prattled on, an old black-and-white movie extolling the virtues of some courageous Indian farmer in his fight against the wicked landowner.

Popular scenario number 5, from memory.

I paid it no attention.

I lay there, thinking of where my road had led me and where I would rather have been. I tried to list my problems.

I was indentured for life to an organisation that offered only two exit plans. Cremation or burial.

I was about to be drafted into a war where I was enemy number one and would probably not survive.

I could not go to the police for help given the nature of my employment.

The woman I wanted to share my life with would never accept me as her partner as long as I stayed with my current employer.

She was consumed with sorrow for her ailing father. Her life would have to revolve around him until his suffering ended.

My colleague Imtiaz wanted to hurt me.

Most worryingly, I had no means by which to run away from all this, to catch a plane to the Bahamas or Madagascar or Morocco.

Everything I had earned was spent.

I had no escape. I just had a great wardrobe.

Why do we always learn the importance of thrift late in our lives?

Any way I looked at it, there was only one solution.

I had to get out of the organisation alive, defuse the tension between our two organisations, help Bunty find peace thereby easing Kalpana's pain, make some money and start all over again.

A complete reshoot of the last nine years.

For the first time in my life I had to acknowledge that life and the movies were not always the same.

If what I have listed above were happening in a movie, our hero would have been struck by some brilliant yet simple plan and in 20 minutes of screen time, his problems would be over.

But this was reality.

No fairy godmother, no magic lamp, no genie, no divine inspiration, no guardian angel.

I walked around my little room, cursing myself for having allowed myself to have got into the situation I was in.

It seemed hopeless. Truly hopeless.

I sat on the edge of my bed, remote in hand, channel surfing at random, paying no heed to the action taking place on the screen.

Then, I heard a voice.

No, sorry, too dramatic.

There was no divine intervention or voice of God or guardian angel. It was simply a rich, chocolatey human voice that brought back memories of happy times in my village, sitting outdoors in our makeshift theatre, watching our battered old TV night after night, a childhood free of all cares or concerns.

The memory of that voice drew my attention to the picture on the screen.

A strong, proud face. High cheekbones, powerful flashing eyes.

Bunty Bhaskar truly had been a handsome man.

I watched on. I remembered the movie. *Man of Honour.*

As I had mentioned to Bhaskar the first night I met him, it had been one of my favourites.

His performance drew me in.

I watched for an hour as the movie drew to its dramatic end.

A man whose family had been killed by an evil mill owner, seeking vengeance. His fight against injustice. The struggle against a heartless and corrupt system.

The explosive last scene, where Bunty's character finally faces up to his demons and with extraordinary courage puts an end to them, was still as powerful and moving as I remembered it from all those years ago.

The man really could act.

I watched transfixed, tears streaming down my face.

Finally, it ended. The credits rolled on, but I still sat there, thinking about what I had just seen.

I remembered what an assistant director had once said to me.

'There are no new ideas. Find an old one and dress it up anew.'

I stood up like a man in a trance, got dressed and headed out to Saraswati.

My head pounded relentlessly. My eyes burned raw.

The monsoon flu, I thought.

I would go see Salim the chemist, see if he had the solution to my predicament.

I would then go see my friend Rashid to see where the future could take me.

Finally, I had to talk to Kalpana.

I had to get her approval.

I had decided that if she agreed, I would do something I had never done before.

My way of living life, up to that moment, had been to let fate present me with an opportunity and leave me to make my decision.

This time, I would have to create the opportunities myself and leave fate to determine my future.

16

LET THE TENSION BUILD

Two days had passed since I had shared my idea with Kalpana, and after a lot of talk, some hesitation and much persuasion, got her agreement.

Two days were now left before Salgaonkar's deadline expired.

Two days to war.

At 9 a.m in the morning, I parked Saraswati outside the Bhaskar residence and rang the doorbell. Bunty himself seldom left his home before early afternoon. Kalpana started work at 9 a.m. sharp every day.

Today was one of her regular monthly 'inspiration shopping' trips on behalf of the wardrobe department.

She would hire a car for the day, and I would accompany her all over the city to all her usual haunts.

My job was to carry the suitcases she filled with the items she wanted, to pack clothes for her, to fetch her drinks when she was thirsty, to make sure she was not bothered by beggars and urchins.

I told you. Being a PA is hell!

Designer showrooms, sari shops, *salwar* and *khameez* outlets, large multi-storey mega-marts, tiny specialist boutiques, we went everywhere. From chic stores in 5-star hotels to street bazaars where clothes and fabrics were strewn over pushcarts and wheeled through the streets, she spent the morning looking, feeling, discarding, combining, imagining and finally, selecting.

One of the privileges of being a movie producer was you never actually had to buy anything.

Merchants and designers were only too happy to lend you items on consignment, for approval.

You only paid for the items you kept and simply returned the rest.

Such is the power of the silver screen that the merest possibility of a 'special' mention in the credits or a 'with thanks to...' turned even the hardest-nosed retailers into giggling stargazers.

I, as always, packed her selections into the large suitcases we used for these trips and loaded them into the car.

Finally, at 2 p.m., she felt she had enough ideas and stimuli for her session with the costume and wardrobe people.

At 3.15 p.m., we drove up to the gates of Glorious Cine Studios. I asked the driver to stop so I could check whether Krishna had any news for me. He had become an important ally over the last few years, and I knew that if any of

Salgaonkar's men came sniffing around the studio, he'd be the one to let me know.

I could not ask him out loud in Kalpana's presence.

The last thing she needed was more to worry about.

Providentially though and due to the fact that we are a nation of over 1500 languages and seldom meet another Indian who speaks one's own mother tongue, we are also masters of the art of nonverbal communication.

We may share no common mode of speech but every single Indian, whichever part of the country he be from, speaks the same eye-roll, head tilt, chin waggle, nostril flare, forehead wrinkle, ear lobe pull, teeth suck and lip purse.

So, as he approached the car, I lifted an eyebrow.

He stopped and slanted his chin left.

I wrinkled my forehead and jerked my head upwards.

He wobbled his head.

Message received. No enemy forces sighted yet.

We drove the kilometre or so from the security gates to the studio.

We got out, and I lugged the suitcases of clothes up the stairs into the production office.

At 3.30 p.m., the others had assembled there, and the wardrobe planning session had begun.

As the discussion turned to cuffs, collars, cuts and colours, I got back into the hire car on my way to Bunty Bhaskar's house to pick up the man himself.

At the gate, I chatted briefly with Krishna.

I asked if he expected a busy night ahead of him.

He doubted it he said. No night shoots on the schedule.

Next, I got the driver to drive towards Andheri, stopping at a DVD shop to buy a movie I intended to watch that evening.

From there, I called in at Salim's Chemist shop to pick up the medication I had ordered earlier. We chatted. I comforted him with the thought that his troubles would soon be over and left.

At 5 p.m. I drove back to Bunty's house.

There I dismissed the hire car and driver and brought Saraswati round to the front door, awaiting Bunty to emerge.

While I waited, I made a telephone call.

The man at the other end was at first surprised, disbelieving, unwilling to listen, but I promised him success beyond the dreams of an ordinary character actor like himself.

Finally, after receiving all the assurances I could give and carried away by visions of himself as a major player in a starring role, he agreed.

I gave him explicit instructions on where and most importantly, when.

I stressed the importance of punctuality.

One could not keep a major star and producer like Bunty Bhaskar waiting.

The great man's name was the final bit of convincing he needed.

Before he hung up, I reminded him of the importance of Gandhiji's dictum that all Indians should help each other.

I left him expectant and excited, counting down the hours to impending stardom.

At 5.30 p.m., Bhaskar emerged. I could see he was having difficulty walking, unsteady on his feet.

I have to admit that he looked terrible.

The agony in his head was now playing out openly on his face. He stumbled over his words. His hands shook, and his breathing sounded heavy and laboured.

He climbed into Saraswati, and we started for the studio.

'I am really sorry about what is happening, Bhaskar sir,' I said to him while we were stopped at traffic lights.

'So, Kalpana has told you. I thought she would. She seems to have grown very fond of you.'

I smiled. 'I think she is a wonderful person, sir, I really...'

He raised a hand, stopping me in my tracks.

'Stop here, Ricki. Just stop. I have something to say to you. Kalpana is a modern Indian woman with ridiculous modern ideas about equality and egalitarianism. She does not believe in the position one's birth puts one in. She does not care about caste or creed or even religion. But I do.

I like you, Ricki. I depend on you, and I certainly trust you. But I am a Hindu traditionalist.

Kalpana may not care that you are really just a rickshaw driver of lower caste, but I can never forget it, and for that reason I can never allow you to get close to my daughter.

Is that understood?'

My God, the man was hard to like.

I sighed in sorrow but said nothing.

This is conventional India.

Happiness has to come second to tradition.

A little further on, I heard him groan.

I turned around to see him holding his head in his hands.

'The pain is really bad today, Ricki. Have you something special to help me through the evening?'

And there you have the modern India.

A nation where progress encourages us to rely on each other as much as tradition allows us to revile each other.

I kept my tone as steady as I could.

'I am expecting a delivery of our very best stock very soon. Really special stuff. I will bring it to you later tonight.'

'Thank you, Ricki…I am really grateful to you.' And in an instant I had turned from unacceptable life form back to indispensable friend.

Life in the service industry!

At 6 p.m., we drove through the studio gates again.

Krishna pursed his lips. I tilted my chin. We exchanged an upward toss of the head.

All was calm.

I accompanied Bunty Bhaskar up the stairs to his office. In truth, I am not sure he could have managed on his own. His legs seemed to wobble under him. He tried to drag himself along the bannister, but there too his strength was failing him.

I helped him to his couch, and he immediately started to pour himself a drink from the decanter placed on a tray next to him.

His long night of pain relief had begun.

Kalpana tucked a blanket around his legs and then turned to me. She pointed to the suitcases of clothes I had lugged up the stairs earlier in the day.

'Those can go back home, Ricki. We'll return them tomorrow.'

Once again, I dragged the suitcases down the stairs and put them in Saraswati. It was a squeeze, but it left just enough room for Kalpana to sit comfortably.

I went back for Kalpana. 'Ready when you are, madam,' I said.

She gathered her handbag and followed me to the door.

There she stopped, turned back and walked up to Bunty, now holding onto his glass with two trembling hands.

Gently, she ran a hand along his cheek then bent over and gave him a slow, lingering kiss on the top of his head.

He looked up at her in surprise.

'Goodbye, Father,' she said to him, in the most tender voice I had ever heard her use.

Then, before more emotion could start to cloud her eyes, she turned and walked out the door and down to the waiting rickshaw.

'Don't forget tonight, Ricki,' Bhaskar pleaded, eyes screwed shut, fighting off the pain.

As the clock in his office sounded the 6:30 p.m. chimes, I too turned and left him there, alone and in need of the comfort that no human being could give him.

At the gates I bade Krishna goodnight.

'I will see you tomorrow,' I told him.

He smiled, no doubt thinking of the extra Mahatma magic he would receive the next day.

At 7.00 p.m. I dropped Kalpana home and took her suit-cases into her house.

I then turned back towards my rickshaw, ready for the journey home.

She thanked me. I wished her a pleasant evening.

Kalpana watched from the door as I got in and started the engine.

Then she pulled the door shut behind her and was gone.

Kalpana had settled in for the night.

Mine was now beginning.

17

BUILD TO THE CLIMAX

I spent the rest of the evening in my apartment behind the office, preparing for the night ahead.

I checked over and over again that I had everything I needed on me.

I wore one of my English sports coats with pockets large enough to hold everything it had to.

On the other side of the door, in the office, I could hear Imtiaz and Mr Arif.

Every evening, Mr Arif sat in the office writing up his books, locking away the day's take, making note of client orders, stock sold and the monies collected.

On the other side of the desk, Imtiaz took phone calls from clients, counted out the bricks that were to be delivered and gave the other drivers their delivery instructions.

This was our office life, and it played out every day, seven days a week.

Finance and Sales, working side by side, as in happy offices everywhere.

Then, on the dot of 9.00 p.m. every evening, Mr Arif would put his books into the office safe, collect the empty tiffin in which Mrs Arif provided his daily lunch, sling his hessian satchel over his shoulder, bid us goodnight and ride his bicycle away into the night.

Imtiaz usually stayed on until 9.30 most evenings when he would lock the drawers on his side of the desk, place whatever stock had been left unsold into the office safe, seal it up for the night, leave the office without so much as a parting word and drive away.

Their nightly routine. It never varied.

Tonight, I sat on my bed, checking the time on my wristwatch.

At 8.45 p.m. I pocketed the screwdriver I had taken earlier from Saraswati's tool kit and walked into the office.

Mr Arif noticed the special effort I'd made with the English coat and Italian loafers.

'Big night, Mr Ricki?' he asked, a big toothy grin on his face.

'A man cannot live on work alone Arif sahib,' I responded.

He giggled. 'I remember, I remember.'

The grin had turned into a look of absolute lechery.

Really, is there anything more repugnant than an amoral accountant?

I said goodnight to both men and left the office. Imtiaz watched me leave.

Once past the main entrance and out of sight of the two men, I turned sharply left towards the part of the compound where our vehicles were parked when not on the road.

No light fell on this side of the holding area.

Saraswati stood there in the dark, cloaked in shadows.

'Not tonight old friend,' I whispered, as I made my way past her and walked on towards Imtiaz's battered old Premier Padmini.

I reached for the handle on the boot lid and sure enough, as I had suspected, it was still faulty. The broken lock closed adequately but not completely. It hooked, but it did not latch.

I opened the boot and climbed inside.

I lowered the boot lid on myself and heard the click of the faulty catch as it met the broken locking mechanism. Then I curled myself into as small a ball as I could, shut my eyes and listened to the silence.

I tried to shut out all images of Imtiaz's father, Imran, being sawn in half and stuffed into this same space. For once, being small was better than being tall.

Soon enough I heard the squeak of Mr Arif's bicycle chain as he rode out of the compound and presumably into the arms of Mrs Arif.

Silence fell again.

Then, sure enough, some 45 minutes later, footsteps approached the car.

The door opened. Padmini's ancient suspension sighed as the driver got into the car. The car started, and we were off.

We jolted and jarred through Mumbai's streets for what seemed an eternity.

It helped that I am slight of build.

It did not help that I am also incredibly bony.

Every pothole sent me hurtling up against the inside of the boot lid.

Every time we braked, I hit my face on the back of car.

My knees and elbows bore the brunt of it, banging and bumping against the cold metal of Padmini's boot space.

In any other car the noises emanating from the back would have alerted the driver that something was amiss.

The Padmini though, that marvel of mechanical malfeasance that she is, travelled with her own orchestra.

Tonight's program presented such a crescendo of squeaks, rattles, thumps and bangs, no one could have noticed the extra commotion coming from her boot.

I wasn't just being turned and tossed, I was also being gassed and gagged. Filthy, oily exhaust fumes seeped through the rust holes on the floor of the boot and into my lungs.

By the time we finally stopped, I was bruised, battered and very nearly physically sick.

Definitely not the best plan I had ever conceived.

I heard voices over the idling engine.

'Good evening, sir,' said Krishna.

'Salaam, Krishna,' replied Imtiaz, before driving through the gates and eventually parking in some dark corner of the lot.

You cannot rely on much in this world. But as any Indian movie buff will tell you, you can always rely on love.

From 10 p.m. to midnight Kalpana had said.

Sure enough Imtiaz's heart had got me into the studio on time and unnoticed.

I heard him walk away and waited until all was silent again.

Then, taking the screwdriver out of my pocket, I prised open the boot release. The lid lifted open, and I stepped out, closing it again behind me.

When no night shoots were scheduled the lot was a deserted space.

I knew where Imtiaz and Rosie met every evening, so I walked around the grounds, away from the bench they sat on, making my way eventually to Studio 6.

I checked my watch. It was now 10.20 p.m.

Studio 6 was in darkness, except for the light in the window that told me Bunty was still in his office.

I walked up the stairs and let myself in.

Bunty Bhaskar was stretched out on the couch, the decanter of whisky near empty.

Drunk though he was, he tried to rise to his feet when he saw me.

'At last,' he gasped, 'at last. Quickly, Ricki, give it to me. Please. Now!'

I took the small parcel from my pocket and handed it to him.

He looked down at the square box in his hands.

'This looks different? What is this "Compliments of Govind Industries?"'

'I told you, sir, this is special stuff.'

He fumbled while trying to open it. His fingers seemed to disobey his commands. The box fell to the floor.

'Here,' I said, 'let me do it for you.'

I carefully opened the box, laying its lid on the desk.

I poured some of the powder onto the desktop.

Then, taking a card out of my pocket, I cut him two short lines of heroin.

Like a starving man, he inhaled the lines greedily.

I watched him closely.

I saw the initial rush of euphoria hit him.

His eyes narrowed. A small smile broke out over his face. The pain was receding.

'More! One more!' he ordered.

'Not yet, sir. Enjoy this now, and in a little while, you may have the rest.'

For the next hour, I sat with him and watched as, at first, the euphoria turned into anxiety, and his body started shaking and twitching. Then, his breathing slowed to almost a standstill, and he lay back with a sigh, a contented, peaceful look on his face.

At 11.30 p.m., I started to make the preparations I had been planning.

I put the DVD into the player in the office and turned it on. The movie started playing. I turned down the lights and sat in the darkness, watching one of the greats of Indian cinema giving the performance of his life.

Around 12.30 a.m., I knew Imtiaz and his lady would be gone.

Except for Krishna and his two assistants at the gate, a distant kilometre away, Bunty Bhaskar and I were alone on the lot.

Finally, Bunty stirred.

His eyes had trouble focussing. His mind was clouded by the drink and drugs. He sat up slowly, and I turned up the volume on the TV.

He watched. As he did, tears formed in his eyes.

He watched himself, a young, handsome man of honour as he was then.

He started crying.

For a time gone. A youth lost. A life ended.

'Look at me, Ricki,' he said, turning to me.

'Look at what I was.'

'That man,' he pointed at the screen, 'had everything. Millions adored him, just wanted a glimpse of him.

He could do anything. The world was his.

Look at me now.

A cartoon of a man.

Unable to walk, unable to stand tall, unable to live.'

With that, he put his head into his hands and started sobbing.

I looked at my watch.

Almost 1 a.m.

This time I cut him two long lines of powder, more than the amount he would normally take, then helped him to the table and watched as he sniffed it up greedily.

He sat back.

'Time may have passed, sir,' I said, 'but something has not changed. You are still the finest, most powerful actor in India. Look at the screen, sir.'

The movie was winding up to the final climactic moment.

'Who else could have played that scene? Who else could have turned a movie about vengeance and vigilantes into a box-office hit?'

'Yes, yes,' he said, eyes fixed on the screen.

'I was good. I was...the best!'

Drugged and foggy as he was, in a low voice he started to mouth the lines he had spoken to camera some 40 years ago. They came to him as naturally as songs to a bulbul.

I looked at my watch.

Time for the final shot.

I prayed that the timings would work out. There could be no retakes.

'Please, Bunty sir,' I begged. 'Please one last time, play the role again. Just for me. Show me the actor that all Bollywood bowed before.'

He looked at me, and slowly, a small smile broke out over his face.

Shakily, he rose to his feet.

He stood proud, feet apart.

As I had suspected, narcotics may well destroy the body, but they could not diminish the ego. Effortlessly, he began the very Bollywood monologue that would bring the movie to an end. Word for word, action for action, he played out for me in the office, the scene playing out on the TV.

'You have taken everything from me. My family. My very life. God teaches us to forgive, but I am no God. I am but a man!'

I heard the car draw up to the car park outside. He was on time. I breathed out in relief.

Bunty, now consumed by the role he was playing seemed unaware of anything happening around him. He was lost in another world, another time, another life.

His voice roared powerfully.

'There is only one way to deal with a dog like you. Others tremble at your feet, but I will not. I stand before you tonight, not a man defeated, but a man victorious. For tonight, I will take from you the one thing you cannot buy. Tonight, I will take your life!'

I watched the man on the screen.

As he raised his clenched arm towards the villain, so too did the man in the room.

As the young Bunty's lips quivered with emotion and tears rolled down his cheeks, so too with the aged Bunty before me. The synchronisation was eerie.

I heard the creak of feet upon the stairs. He had followed my instructions perfectly.

I pulled the final prop out of my waistband.

I placed Avzal's blue pistol in Bunty's outstretched arm.

'Don't worry, sir,' I assured him. 'Only blanks.'

But Bunty Bhaskar was gone. Before me stood Shiva the destroyer. All powerful, righteous and driven to exact the vengeance that was so rightly his.

I gazed quickly at the office door.

On cue, through the glass pane, I saw the silhouette of the man on the stairs get closer. He paused at the door as if listening to the scene being played out inside.

'The law may prosecute me,' the man of honour thundered, lost in his mind, in his own power, 'God may punish me, but I will die happily, victorious, knowing that one less snake, one less dog walks this earth.'

The man at the door knocked.

His sound cut through the tense room like three loud drumbeats.

Bunty, hearing it, turned towards the door as simultaneously the character on the screen turned towards the camera.

'Die swine, and long may you burn in the fires of my hatred!' they both screamed.

The man on the stairs opened the door and stepped into the room.

Both Buntys raised their arms simultaneously and fired three shots.

On screen, all three shots entered the villain's body, killing him instantly.

In real life, the first bullet missed by a metre and broke a glass window on the side of the door.

The second pinged off the doorframe and shattered the empty decanter that stood on the table by the couch.

Fortunately, the third found its mark, burying itself deep into the chest of Shri Nandu Talpade, Area Coordinator, Govind Industries, who first stared down at the red splotch spreading over his shirt and then fluttered to the ground like a 20-rupee kite that has suddenly lost the wind.

I looked at Bunty. He looked like a man in the middle of a hallucination.

'Oh my God, oh my God, what have I done? Ricki, what have I done?'

I ran up to him, took the pistol out of his hand and sat him down at his desk.

'Nothing, Bunty sir, nothing at all. It is all a movie, you have just played out the final scene and shooting is finished. Now, sir, you can rest!'

With that, I poured out the rest of the powder.

'All of it, sir,' I urged him. 'You deserve it.'

He looked up at me, surprised, 'All of it?'

I wondered for a moment if he understood. Did reality cut through the buzzing distortions in his brain?

'It's over sir. Time to wrap,' I whispered to him softly.

Slowly he smiled at me. His eyes shone bright, filled with a contented gleam. Did I see a flash of hope in them somewhere?

He nodded at me slowly, looked down at all the powder that lay there in front of him and without any further hesitation, snorted up all the remaining heroin.

He sat back.

Fentanyl is a synthetic opioid, a hundred times more powerful than straight heroin. Salim had obtained it for me. I had mixed far more than a safe quantity of it into the package that lay open in front of Bunty. His eyes closed, and his breathing came to a near stop.

I sat there with him for an hour or so until I was sure hypoxia had done its job. The slow breathing, so symptomatic of a fentanyl overdose, deprives the brain of the oxygen it needs to keep functioning. If treated quickly, the patient may suffer no more than partial damage. But left like this for an hour, or more, the brain shuts down completely, floating deep into a coma, one that would keep Bunty Bhaskar free of pain, of suffering, for as long as his God chose to let him live.

I arranged the parcel so that the words on the lid were clearly visible.

I laid the card that I had used to cut the heroin for Bunty on top of the box, Nandu Talpade's visiting card that I had taken from Salim.

I slipped the DVD into my pocket.

I then lay Bunty Bhaskar on the floor, pistol in hand, powder sprinkled over his chest.

Where illusion is concerned, art direction is everything.

Finally, it was my turn.

Up to this moment, I had produced and directed the scene. Now I had to step up as performer. My one moment of on-camera glory had arrived.

At 2.30 a.m., I picked up the phone on the desk and pressed the direct dial number to Krishna's security office at the gate. He answered.

I started sobbing into the phone, a handkerchief wrapped around the mouthpiece. I lowered my voice and stuttered out my words, as if overcome by a huge tragedy. In short staccato words I said, 'Come quick...Studio 6. Bring...bring your men. I think...oh God...I think I have killed a man.'

I heard the alarm in Krishna's voice.

'Coming now, Bhaskar sir,' he shouted as I dropped the phone, hoping to simulate the effect of man and instrument crashing to the floor.

I pulled Talpade into the room by his feet. He was already stone cold, his eyes open wide in muted disbelief. I found an evil switchblade in his inside pocket.

I made sure the huge floor-to-ceiling safe was locked. If the police saw its contents, it would just create another problem.

Finally, with only a few moments left before Krishna and his men would cover the kilometre or so from his office to the studio, I turned to say goodbye to Bunty Bhaskar.

His act and his agony were now over.

I waited outside in the shadows of the banyan tree. I watched Krishna and his men run past me and into the studio. I knew the security box would be unattended.

I walked down to the gate. No guards in sight.

I paused, looked back and said a silent goodbye.

At 3.15 a.m., I walked out the gate and out of movie land forever.

18

LEAVE NO DRY EYES

For three weeks I laid low in my tiny apartment. The office was locked and closed. The drivers given three weeks paid leave. Imtiaz, Mr Arif and all of our organisation employees had been told to stay off the streets, to keep hidden because, for three weeks, the biggest scandal to ever rock Bollywood took Mumbai by storm. I read all the newspapers, watched all the news reports on TV to stay abreast of proceedings.

One of India's greatest ever actors, caught in a web of deceit, drugs and duplicity, had shot and killed a drug dealer employed by Govind Industries.

In a cruel twist of fate, the drugs supplied to him by that dealer had been cut with a lethal synthetic opioid, and Bunty Bhaskar, one-time hero of the masses, had been reduced to the mental level of a Bengan Bhaji. Permanently!

The city and its denizens were up in arms.

How useless were our authorities to allow Bollywood, the land where good must win and endings must be happy, to get so embroiled in such ferocious and bloody villainy?

How were criminals allowed to become producers, their black money used to finance sweet, G-rated family features? How widespread and unchecked was our drug problem? How high up the ladder does this corruption run? How easy was it to buy lethal drugs?

Editors wrote furious opinion pieces decrying the state of lawlessness we now had to live with.

Opposition politicians pulled out their soap boxes and gave long, emotion-filled speeches about our ineffective government, ineffective leadership and ineffectual police force.

Powerful producers and movie stars pounced on the Sheriff and Mayor of Mumbai, demanding greater protection from criminal gangs and security for themselves.

The governor of Maharashtra assured us that the police would leave no stone unturned in capturing those responsible. He was even photographed visiting a comatose Bunty Bhaskar in hospital.

So great was the outcry, the Mumbai police force finally had to do something.

They arrested and charged Mr Govind Salgaonkar of Govind Industries, whose package of contaminated drugs was found on Bunty Bhaskar's desk, with importing, supplying and distributing hard drugs.

His employees and distributors were rounded up and thrown into Tihar jail. His operatives were fleeing the city, his network either incarcerated or in Thailand.

Last heard, his elder brother and CEO of the organisation, Mr Narendra Salgaonkar, had flown to the Maldives from where he was negotiating settlement terms with various countries previously open to harbouring India's garbage. Unfortunately for him, being a Hindu, even Pakistan, usually so open to greeting and garlanding any person seen as being an enemy of India (any person with sufficient funds of course), had turned its back on him.

The police were steamrolling through Salgaonkar territory. Within two weeks his empire was as good as finished.

Word had come down that Bade Mian had decreed that while this police 'clean up' was taking place, we too would cease all business activity.

A blow to the bottom line of course, but a wise business move.

After weeks of no new stock on the market, sales would boom at an even greater rate.

Early morning on the 15th day of the raging scandal, Bunty Bhaskar died.

His doctors informed the world that Bunty Bhaskar had, for some time, bravely battled with a glioblastoma multiforme, a debilitating cancer, but had finally and inevitably succumbed to it. His brain tumour was listed as the cause of death. The dangerous narcotic overdose had put him in a coma, but it had not killed him. Most importantly, the doctor assured us that in his final days, being in a coma, Bunty Bhaskar was in absolutely no discomfort and no distress.

The city was united in its grief. More pressure was put on the police to wipe out Salgaonkar's network.

That evening, his cremation was attended by hundreds, with further thousands lining the streets leading to Mahim crematorium, hoping to get one final sight of the great man and the other stars who would be turning up for the funeral.

Politicians, high-ranking police officials, captains of industry, sportsmen, professionals from all walks of life and most of Bollywood turned up to jostle for seats and make the most of the photo opportunities on offer.

Actresses who detested the man wiped away tears and presented anguished faces to the assembled media cameras.

Other leading men of his era who hated him for his success, and the roles he took from them, instantly cast themselves as his closest friends, sharing tender anecdotes of the great man's generosity and kindness.

Younger stars added real glamour to the occasion, talking reverentially to the assembled press and citing Bunty Bhaskar as the inspiration for their careers.

Solemnity meets star power.

No one does funerals like Bollywood.

I stood silently at the back of the crematorium. As his body was borne towards the flames, I saw Kalpana wipe her eyes.

But she looked calm, relaxed.

Her father had finally found the peace she had so wanted for him.

That evening at sunset, she and I waded out into the shallow waters at Juhu beach, and as per our tradition, released his ashes into the water. They floated away towards the setting sun.

Quickly, I opened the tiny parcel I had brought with me and sprinkled some white powder into the water alongside his ashes.

Bunty Bhaskar would want for nothing in the afterlife.

The next day a leading weekend newspaper ran a lengthy interview with Kalpana Bhaskar, the grieving daughter. In it, she revealed the background to Bunty's illness, the agony he had suffered.

While she was angry that the drugs supplied to her father by these 'scoundrels' were tainted, she professed relief that he had been spared more pain towards the end.

'He was at peace,' she said. 'The final days brought him no further suffering.' Perhaps, she suggested, that was God's reward for having led the disciplined and righteous life he had.

I suppose it is every child's right to glorify (and fiction-alise) the memory of a parent deceased.

On the final day of our self-imposed isolation, three weeks from that eventful night, Avzal Bhai rang to summon me to Sheik Mohsin's office. Imtiaz was sent to pick me up. We rode towards Behndi Bazaar in near silence, hostility emanating from the man like heat from a charcoal burner.

I decided to try for a rapprochement one last time.

'Will Bade Mian be there?' I asked.

'Fool,' he answered, 'only the top two or three people in the organisation ever get to meet Bade Mian. For someone that senior, secrecy is security. I have worked here since I was a boy, and I have never even seen so much as one hair on Bade Mian's head.

You think such a big boss would want to meet a frog like you?

Today, we are getting our new orders.

What we need to do to take over as much of Salgaonkar's territory as we can.'

This was not good news to me. The future I'd been planning was based more on disappearance than domination.

Imtiaz must have read my thoughts. He looked at me from the corner of his eye.

'Don't think you can ever run away from us, frog. You try and I swear I will slit you like a Bombay Duck from your skull down to your arse. Trust me on that!'

More bad news.

Nothing ruins a gentle sail away into the sunset like a knife protruding from the sphincter.

Would no one ever rid me of this pesky Pathan?

Finally, we pulled up outside the old building where I had been accepted into the organisation all those years ago. We were greeted at the door by the same giggling, wriggling, fat madam as before, only now several years saggier and uglier.

I walked past the ladies, down the corridor and to the door of Sheik Mohsin's office. I entered when it was opened. Imtiaz followed me in.

Sheik Mohsin, Avzal Bhai and four other lieutenants were crowded round the desk with the forest scene carving on the front. I saw a large map of Mumbai on the table.

Imtiaz pulled me to a corner of the room as Sheik Mohsin issued instructions for the group.

'Avzal, you now have all of Bandra, Khar, Santa Cruz all the way to Juhu. Inshan Ali, take Andheri and Vile Parle up to Sahar airport.

Ridwan, you run Jogeshwari to Bhandup West, across to Mulund.

Ibrahim, I'm giving you Madh to Thane, including Kandivili and Goregaon.

And you, Papa Mian; Borivili, Gorai and Kasarvadavali.'

Salgaonkar's territory was being carved up faster than a goat at an *iftaar*.

Sheik Mohsin was wasting no time in making sure that while Salgaonkar's forces were taking cover, we were taking over.

'Is everyone clear?' he asked, sitting back in his expansive leather chair with the air of a man who is just about to double his empire.

The men nodded.

Mohsin was not done though.

'I want to be very clear about how we're going to do this.

We will do this by winning friends, not intimidating people. Bade Mian feels it is time we start to change our sales techniques as the world is changing about us. Learn from the telecoms and cable TV operators. Think about offering a signing up discount. A switchover bonus. Free gifts with every upgrade to larger orders. A 1-800 line in case of emergencies. Use your initiative.

The old days are gone. We must become the business that best understands the new India. One where the customer is king.

You will smile. Show your gums not your guns. Take a box of *mithai* for the family. You will persuade gently. You will not spill any blood.

If people seem hesitant, remind them calmly that we are the only source of product at the moment. If they wish to retire and sit at home raising grandchildren, we wish them well. But if they want to stay in business and make money, they have to deal with us.

Start with Salgaonkar's larger distributors. Get them on side. They will bring their dealers and street sales force with them.

Get your men to talk to every *bidi* shop, every building security guard, every office peon they can. Hit every sweatshop, illegal factory, backstreet drinks hall, gambling den.

Find the misery gentlemen, and there you will find the money.'

The men all nodded, clearly impressed by the scale of the sales drive being mounted.

'And one more thing. You will naturally come across some of Salgaonkar's men. The foot soldiers who do not have the funds to escape the police net, the junior sales staff and the assistant managers who have just enough to be allowed to stay hidden. There are still plenty of small fry out there. You may not slaughter them! Do you understand, Ibrahim, not even a simple amputation!

I understand that this is a change from our previous policy of behead and be happy, but now, instead of scaring them off, you will offer them the opportunity to work for you.

You are authorised to offer them up to 15% more than their last salary to move to our organisation. You will let them continue to run their customers as they always have, but now, for us, under you.'

I saw the men look at each other uncertainly.

Ridwan, the wickedest-looking of all, thick glasses over small beady eyes, spoke for them.

'But, Boss, they are mostly all Hindus!'

The others nodded, clearly appalled at the thought that their armies, so racially pure until now, would soon have to accept bell-ringing, mantra-chanting vegetarians.

Sheik Moshin stood up from his chair, drew himself to his full height and faced his men head-to-head.

'Bade Mian strongly believes that the time has come for us to stand up for India. As our government continues to ignore the basic tenets of our Indian Constitution, it is essential that truly patriotic businesses like ours stand up for our country.

Gentlemen, we are going secular!

After all, cash knows no caste system.

There are no tribal distinctions to turnover.

Bade Mian wants us to become a tolerant, broad-minded organisation where all Indians are equals.

No sales will be considered untouchable.

We will lead Indian business to a new future.

In our India the Temple of Transaction and the Mosque of Monetary Gain will stand side by side, proud, equal partners!'

And you thought I overdid it!

Whoever writes his speeches, I thought, needs a lesson in moderation. Or, better still, another job.

The men loved it, though.

Spontaneous applause broke out. Sheik Mohsin almost took a bow before he remembered his role and collected himself.

Finally, fired by enthusiasm for their new-found mantra of fraternal love, the men filed out excitedly.

Only Avzal, Imtiaz and I remained.

Sheik Mohsin turned towards me. His eyes were fixed on me, hard and unforgiving.

I had been pushed down onto one of the settees while Mohsin had been instructing the troops. Now, I felt Avzal's heavy hand on my shoulder, holding me down.

Mohsin picked up a wicked-looking letter opener, long and razor-sharp, and picking at his nails, he advanced upon me.

'Now,' he said to me, with the hungry look of a street dog that's just spotted a discarded *seekh kebab* wrapper, 'what are we going to do about you? You have let us down. You were sent to look after one of our most important clients, and he is now dead. You allowed Salgaonkar to sell him tainted drugs resulting in a police operation that nearly brought an end to our business. It's all blown into an almighty mess. You have failed us, Ricki,' he placed the tip of his letter opener under my left eye, 'and now, it's time to pay!'

19

MAKE THE LAST REEL MEMORABLE

Ok. The last shot.

Time for the superhero to show his powers.

I spread my arms and stepped off the ledge.

'You have misunderstood the situation, sir. Everything that happened, happened exactly to plan. I did not let you down, Sheik Mohsin. I have actually made you even more powerful.'

The letter opener paused in mid-air. The cataract operation could wait.

Power was just too important, a commodity not to be dismissed lightly.

'What nonsense are you going to serve up now?' Avzal asked from behind me, his voice shaking in anger. 'You could not know what happened that night? The police and the news-papers are clear that only Bunty Bhaskar and Nandu Talpade were there that night. No one else!'

'They are wrong, sir. I know exactly what happened that night because you see, I was there with them, right to the moment when Mr Bhaskar fired the gun.'

Forget pins, you could have heard a hair drop.

Both surgeon and theatre nurse looked as if they had been smacked in the face. Of all the protestations they may have expected, this was not one.

Avzal spoke first.

'Then why have the police not arrested you? None of your filmy dialogue now, Ricki. Just the truth. What the hell happened?'

And....action!

'As you know, sir, Salgaonkar's men were threatening all our contacts. Scaring them into submission.

Mr Bhaskar is one of our best clients, and the studio is one of our best profit centres. So I was not surprised when they contacted Mr Bhaskar and tried to twist his arm.

That evening, I left the studio around 6.30 p.m. with Miss Kalpana, drove her home then went back to our office. Imtiaz and Mr Arif were there of course and saw me go to my apartment and stay there until about 8.45 p.m.'

Avzal looked at Imtiaz who nodded.

Miss Kalpana, had asked me to escort her to the movies that night. I often drove her around in the evenings. Mr Bhaskar felt it was safer for her.

She will, of course, vouch for this if you feel you need to ask her.

As I was driving to Miss Kalpana's house, I got a call from Mr Bhaskar.

He sounded angry, agitated.

Nandu Talpade had rung him to say that he would be dropping round to see Mr Bhaskar that night to "make him an offer he could not refuse".

'Mr Bhaskar was surprised and wanted to know what was going on.

So, I told him everything.

Salgaonkar's move on our business, their attempt to steal our clients, the possibility of war between our two companies, everything.

I tried to dissuade Mr Bhaskar from seeing Talpade. "He is a dangerous man. Do not antagonise him," I said.

But Mr Bhaskar was determined to stand up to him, to send Talpade off with "a flea in his ear and a boot mark on his behind", as he put it.'

Sheik Mian looked surprised.

'I never realised Bunty Bhaskar was a brave man.'

I jumped in.

'Not courage so much, sir, as loyalty.

You see, Mr Bhaskar's relationship with us was based on more than just business. It was based on friendship. His friendship with Avzal Bhai.

He once said to me, "Avzal has looked out for me since we were boys. He protected me when I was threatened by bullies, befriended me when no one in our neighbourhood would. I will never betray his trust by going behind his back to deal with his enemies." '

Avzal looked at me, a hint of uncertainty in his eyes.

Needy, greedy Bunty Bhaskar showing loyalty?

I played my trump card.

'He even told me that Avzal Bhai had actually helped start him on his career by…eh…"persuading" the judges of an inter-collegiate drama competition to award Mr Bhaskar the best actor award.'

Avzal gave a little start here. That little kernel of historical fact seemed to have silenced him. I saw him turn his eyes away from me and look into the distance.

I presumed he was fondly recalling his first youthful foray into felony.

No one interrupted, so I continued.

'Mr Bhaskar then asked me for something that I did not expect. "Be here tonight by midnight, Ricki, and bring a gun. Just as a prop, you understand.

If I wave it around a bit it may help to show this man I am serious. It may even scare him off."

I protested strongly, but he would not budge.

It sounded to me like Mr Bhaskar had written a dramatic role for himself and nothing was going to stop him from playing it.'

Here, I saw Avzal give a little nod. This Bunty he knew!

'I could of course have ignored this request.

But as I thought about it, there were two very good reasons for doing as Mr Bhaskar asked.

Firstly of course, the sight of a gun might just have set Talpade back a bit, preventing him from physical violence towards Mr Bhaskar. Avzal Bhai had instructed me at the very start that I was to look after Mr Bhaskar, to do as he wanted. Of course, I was not going to disobey that order now at the first hint of trouble.'

I stopped there, worried that I had laid on the dutiful dog bit too thick, but I heard no rumblings from the front row, so I continued.

'My second reason for being there was even more compelling.

What if something went wrong?

Mr Bhaskar is a man with strong dramatic flair.

What if, in his intoxicated state, he decided that the scene demanded more than just the brandishing of a gun and would play more realistically if he actually fired it?

I didn't care if he actually managed to shoot Talpade, he'd be doing us a great service, but what if he shot himself?

Or worse still, what if the security men who patrol the lot heard the shots and burst into the office? Or if someone called the police?

We would have been in real trouble.'

Sheik Mohsin sat up.

'We? Why would we have been in trouble if Bhaskar shot one of Salgaonkar's men?'

'Sir, I remembered that by midnight, lost as he is in his private world of pleasure, Mr Bhaskar leaves evidence of our relationship with him lying all around his office.

Powder spilled on his desk, the torn paper wrappers we deliver it in, the inner plastic bags.

I have seen that Imtiaz does not wear gloves when he packs the plastic bags, wraps them in paper and hands them to us drivers.

His fingerprints and our drivers' too, of course, would be all over those packages.

If the police found them, had them tested for prints, we would all be in jail.'

That's when I realised that while I could not control what happened that night between Talpade and Mr Bhaskar, I could make sure that our organisation could not be implicated in any way possible.

I rang Miss Kalapana to say I could not make the movies that night. I told her I had the monsoon flu.

Instead, I had decided to go clean up the office before Mr Bhaskar staged his little scene.

That was the only way I could keep him or our organisation safe.'

'I considered calling Avzal Bhai, but I knew that if he or Imtiaz heard what Mr Bhaskar was planning, they would have rushed in there and shot Talpade themselves.

That would have definitely started a war.

As I see it, sir, in war everyone loses something precious, but no one ever wins anything worth having.'

I stopped again nervously.

Was the devoted corporate philosopher angle just a stretch too far? I wondered.

To my delight I saw Sheik Mohsin actually nod to himself.

I understood then, for the very first time, the power of the storyteller. Why people make up stuff.

Invention is just so invigorating!

I kept rolling.

'I decided that I would take the gun to Mr Bhaskar. I would clean up the office and then stay with him while Talpade was there to make sure no harm came to him.'

I tried here to effect the look of a valiant protector, ready to give up life and limb in the line of duty.

No one does phoney courage better than the inveterate coward.

'Avzal Bhai had left me with a pistol that he said was untraceable and had given me permission to use it if I thought I or any client of ours was in danger. So, I took it with me and headed for the studio.

But I wanted to make sure that my entry went unobserved and that whatever happened, my presence there was known to no one.'

'You see, if things ended badly, shots were fired or someone got hurt, I did not want the security people at the gate telling the police that I had come to see Mr Bhaskar late that night.

I wanted nothing to point the police in our direction.

So I decided to enter the studio on the quiet.'

'Some time back, I heard of a young make-up artist named Rosie, whose boyfriend drove in to meet her at the lot every night at 10 p.m.

I found where this man worked and parked his car.

He is not important, sir, just some lovesick idiot who knew nothing of my plan.

I hid in the back of his car. He drove into the studio lot, and once he had left to go see the girl, I let myself out of the car and up to Mr Bhaskar's office.'

I heard a small gasp from Imtiaz behind me, but the other two were too engrossed to notice.

'When I got to Mr Bhaskar's office, he was asleep on his couch. I could see he had been helping himself to the powder

I had delivered to him the night before, and I knew he would be asleep for at least an hour or two.'

'For the next hour and a half, I started cleaning out his office. I rounded up all the wrapping papers, plastic bags even the plastic letter opener he used to cut the powder. I carried it all to the 24-hour incinerator that the studio operates at the back lot.

I threw them in and watched them burn into ash. Then, I found the set floor manager's vacuum cleaner and vacuumed the floor, the carpet, his desk and even, while he slept through it, Mr Bhaskar's shirt front.

I even found Mr Bhaskar's mobile phone and deleted both my number and Avzal Bhai's number.'

Sheik Mohsin actually looked impressed with this evidence of my diligence. I was looking good for Employee of the Year.

'By the time I was finished, there was nothing there to connect us to the office, to Mr Bhaskar or his ...uh...habits.'

'Finally, at around 12.30 a.m., Mr Bhaskar awoke.
As with all our clients who come down after a pleasurable high, he wanted another parcel immediately.
I told him there was none there.
I needed him sober and thinking straight when Talpade arrived.
I felt we needed to plan our tactics.
Mr Bhaskar, however, would not talk to me.'

'Frantically, he started searching through the room for more of his powder, pulling out drawers, opening filing cabinets and office cupboards.

I begged him to tell me what he planned to do when Talpade arrived.

"I will play it from the heart," he said to me. "You can't rehearse conviction, Ricki, you just have to feel it on the day."'

'At 1 a.m., we heard a car draw up outside.

I knew that for the right price, Krishna at the security gate would let a hungry lion into his children's bedroom. Talpade had arrived.'

'For Mr Bhaskar, hearing the car was like call time.

Immediately he pulled himself together, into the character of the strong, unyielding hero he was going to play.

He asked me to put the gun on the table "so the swine can see I mean business."'

'Talpade entered the office.

A weasly-looking man with a thin moustache. Oily hair. Dark as the bark of a mango tree. Obviously very lower class, sir, these Salgaonkar chaps.

Mr Bhaskar was at his desk. I stood behind him.

Talpade greeted Mr Bhaskar effusively. He looked surprised to find someone else there.

Mr Bhaskar told him I was his PA, and so of course Talpade immediately ignored me.

No one notices a PA, sir.'

'They started to talk. I heard Mr Bhaskar try to tell him that he would never do business with Talpade, but unfortunately by now, Mr Bhaskar was experiencing serious withdrawal symptoms.

His eyes were cloudy and watery. His hands were shaking. His skin pallid and grey. His words were blurred, made little sense.'

'Talpade is an experienced distributor. He recognised the symptoms at once. Immediately he presented Mr Bhaskar with what looked like a small box of *mithai*. "A small sample of goodwill towards you, Bhaskarji," he said.'

'Such is their arrogance, sir, their total indifference, that on the lid they had printed the words "With the Compliments of Govind Industries."'

I saw Sheik Mohsin look up at the ceiling in disgust.

Advertising! Why had he never thought of that himself?

'Mr Bhaskar opened the box, saw the powder within and was like a man possessed.

Immediately he tried to open the packet, but his hands were trembling so much, he could not.

That swine Talpade rushed to do it for him.

He used his own business card to cut one of the longest lines I have ever seen, and before I could stop him, Mr Bhaskar inhaled two long lines of it.

Talpade just stood there, nodding and grinning.'

'I have seen our clients imbibe our product often, and I know their reactions well. But the reaction I saw now was unlike any other I have seen.

He staggered around the room; he shouted and screamed some dialogue from an old movie of his. His entire body was shaking now. He was panting, out of control. He was in another world. Out of his mind.

Something was not right.'

'"What's in the powder?" I asked Talpade. "Is it 100% pure?"'

'"Pure?" he laughed. "Who does pure anymore? It's 50% fentanyl. Cheaper to buy, easier to get and makes the profits better."'

'I knew then we were in trouble. You see, sir, my poor father suffers terribly from arthritis.

The only relief he gets is from fentanyl, which I get from my chemist friend Salim and send to my father.

Salim has warned me about fentanyl.

It is totally synthetic and about 100 times stronger than the pure, natural product we supply.

It is extremely dangerous and can only be taken in very tiny, controlled amounts.

Talpade had just given Mr Bhaskar far, far more than was safe.'

'He was only used to the genuine stuff we sell. Our stock is 100% pure.

It may make us less money than Salgaonkar's adulterated stuff, but, sir, at least our integrity is intact.'

No reaction at this corporate arse lick. Disappointing.

I thought it worth at least a nod of pride.

'"We need to call an ambulance," I said to Talpade.

He immediately pulled out a knife…this knife, sir.'

With that, I dropped the switchblade I had taken from Talpade onto Sheik Mohsin's desk from a height calculated to make a nice loud thump.

They all jumped.

Sound effects are so crucial in creating tension.

'Talpade refused to help.

"An ambulance will lead to too many questions. Just give the old fellow a few minutes. Anyway, who cares about one less old druggie?" he laughed.

"If this old fool goes, there will be another in his place and another."'

Avzal looked up at this, the glint of battle in eyes.

I hit the 'proud employee' button a bit harder.

'No pride in their product and no honour in their dealings, sir.

They really are second-rate people, this Salgaonkar lot.'

Sheik Mohsin was in no mood for corporate chest thumping.

'Finish the story, man. Just tell us what happened.'

You see?

Everyone needs a story to have a proper resolution.

All questions answered, no dramatic suspense to leave you hanging.

When Hollywood finally learns this, they may start to be as successful as Bollywood.

I continued breathlessly.

'Well, I ignored him and rushed for the phone, but Talpade grabbed me and tried to stab me. I held his knife hand at bay, trying hard to fight him off. We tussled for a few minutes, and I must admit, sir, I was not winning. He was bigger and stronger.

Suddenly, there were three loud bangs.'

'In his madness, Mr Bhaskar had seized the gun and started firing indiscriminately.

He kept shouting, "I will never betray Avzal. I will never deal with you rogues."

One bullet broke a window. One shattered his cut-glass whisky decanter. And fortunately for me, the third bullet hit Talpade in the chest, killing him instantly.

Mr Bhaskar just looked stunned. He dropped the gun. Almost immediately his body went into a convulsion of some sort and just fell to the floor as the fentanyl pushed him into some sort of seizure.

I tried to revive him, get him to sit up, but honestly, I knew it was of no use.

His breathing was so shallow, there was almost no breath at all.

Salgaonkar's impure product had kicked in, and I realised that Mr Bhaskar's brain was being deprived of oxygen.

Hypoxia is one of the great dangers of fentanyl. I always warn my father of it.'

'At first, I thought about getting Mr Bhaskar out of there, take him to a hospital and pretend we were never at the studio.

I wondered if I should try and cover everything up.

But then I realised the opportunity that Mr Bhaskar had presented us with.

Salgaonkar is a real nuisance, sir. He has the police in his pocket, so he gets away with almost anything.'

'As I saw it, only a huge scandal would compel the Mumbai police to go after Salgaonkar.

You know how we Indians worship our filmy heroes.

We turn our Gods into movie stars and our movie stars into Gods.

If the people of Mumbai heard that Salgaonkar had corrupted, duped and ruined the life of a great man, an Indian icon, by plying him with lethal, contaminated drugs, I knew there would be a huge outcry.

The politicians and police would have to act!

They would have to go after Salgaonkar.'

'So, I left everything as it was.

I made sure the box with Govind Industries' name was in a place where the police would spot it easily and placed next to it the visiting card that Talpade had used to cut the line.'

'You may think this was heartless of me and callous towards Mr Bhaskar's needs, but actually, sir, it was the opposite. You see, I knew about Mr Bhaskar's illness. His daughter had told me about it some time ago.

I knew that every day he lived was like hell to him.

I knew he was scared of the end, the final suffering and humiliation he might have to suffer. He could not bear the thought of the pain and misery to come in his final few days.'

'He was a hero, sir. I decided he deserved to go heroically.

If they revived him in hospital, he would have been in an even worse state, a vegetable for life.

In the coma, he was at peace. Released from his agony.

So I decided to let him sleep. To do nothing until I was sure he could never be revived.

I let him go and in so doing, take Salgaonkar with him.'

'Finally, pretending to be Mr Bhaskar, I rang Krishna at the security gate and ordered him to come at once.

I then hid behind a banyan tree until he and his men went running past and then simply strolled out of the gates.

That's it, sir.

The full, true story of what happened that night.'

I know, I know!

More holes than a Mumbai highway after the monsoon.

But, as a scriptwriter once told me, when you pitch an idea, the people you need to sell to are not listening to see if they believe in your story, but if you believe in it!

So, I adopted my most sincere and sorrowful expression and waited silently for that all-important first night audience reaction.

20

SET UP THE SEQUEL

For the longest while, absolutely no one spoke.

Imtiaz looked stunned, uncertain of what to think.

Avzal looked angry.
Either at the loss of his friend or having to sit through another truly tedious Ricki tale. I couldn't tell which.

Sheik Mohsin looked into the distance, as if evaluating the story and rating the performance.

Both Avzal and Imtiaz turned to Sheik Mohsin for his response.

Finally he nodded.

'Everything you say matches the newspaper reports and the police version of events. They believe that maddened by bad drugs, Bhaskar shot the deliveryman.

But there are several things that you have done that I do not approve of, Ricki. You took matters into your own hands.

Our organisation believes in dumb obedience, not initiative.

You allowed Talpade to get to Mr Bhaskar who in the end, you chose not to save. You made a decision about a man's life that only his God should make.'

So far, I had to admit, the reviews were not sounding like an extended run.

'However, you did make sure that we were not implicated in any of this mess. And as you figured, the resulting outcry has considerably damaged Salgaonkar's empire.

Someone who has been our sworn enemy for years has fled the country. Most of his top men are in custody. And if we do this right, we stand to double our own territory.

So, all in all, I think you might just have done us a favour. What do you think, Avzal?'

Of course Avzal was never going to contradict his big boss. But something still niggled at him.

'Yes, sir, I agree that he has saved us. But I wonder if by thinking about Mr Bhaskar rather than himself, he could have saved Bunty from turning into a vegetable.'

'Yes, I see that,' Sheik Mohsin agreed, 'but did he do him a favour or not?

You knew Bunty Bhaskar best, Avzal. You tell us.

Would a proud man like him have wanted the pain, the humiliation of his final days, or would he be grateful for a quick, easy release?'

Avzal said nothing. I thought I saw a hint of moisture in his eyes.

Mohsin had the answer he wanted. He turned to the room.

'With Salgaonkar gone, we will have a bumper year this year.

We can put more of our resources into developing our network and our people rather than spending so much of our income on arms and weapons. And of course, this means that you, Avzal, now go from Sales Director to Area Manager of a substantially larger territory. I think Ricki deserves some credit for all this.'

Avzal turned to me as if tussling inside on which was more important to him.

Finally, as I had hoped, financial gain won over friendship lost.

'What do you want, Ricki? More rickshaws to run? More money? In the end, you did the right thing by us. And yes, I think perhaps you did do Bunty a favour.'

Finally, the all-revealing moment had arrived.

Everything I had schemed, cheated and deceived for came down to this moment. Now I would find out whether all the charades, all the lies would get me the one reward I wanted from these men.

'Well, sir, as I said, my father is unable to work his fields. My mother wrote to say that if another harvest failed, we could lose our little farm. That would kill my father.

You have been very good to me sir. Generous and gracious. I have learnt much from my years with you.

But you don't need me anymore. Salgaonkar's territory will soon be yours, and you can deliver your product openly. You don't need four rickety rickshaws to do that for you.

My parents, however, need me more now than ever before. So, I just want to go home.

I want to return to my village and spend my life working the farm, helping my father grow old gracefully and giving my mother the comfort and support she deserves.

Sir, please. I want no money, no promotion, no more rickshaws.

All I ask is that you let me go home.'

I was rather pleased with this.

Nice bit of pathos.

Family duty. Filial responsibility.

And all played with a deft touch. No big wallowing emotion. No histrionics.

So subtle and underplayed, you could have been watching a Scandinavian movie.

I had bet Kalpana that it would work.

Hadn't Sheik Moshin mentioned at our first meeting that those who served the organisation well would benefit from their generosity?

I knew that gratitude, tempered by greed, would soften their hearts.

Sheik Mohsin looked calm, even satisfied.

A man at peace with himself.

Then he just burst out laughing.

He was shaking his head as if in appreciation of the greatest joke ever told.

'Don't be silly, Ricki. I told you on the very first day, when you join us, you join us forever.

No one ever leaves our organisation. It's just not permitted.

But to show you that we appreciate what you have done, we will be generous. You will stay right here, run the narcotics side of the business in North Mumbai under Avzal and spend the rest of your days an employee of this organisation.'

Avzal was smiling and nodding too.

'You are mine forever, Ricki. Don't ever forget that.'

By now my heart was beating furiously.

I had failed!

All that plotting, planning, conniving, all for nothing.

I would never get Kalpana. Never be free. Never be my own man again.

I was going to be a criminal, a drug dealer for life.

The blood was pounding in my head, crashing loudly in my ears.

I suddenly realised the crashing was actually the crash of the office door being flung open.

The fat madam, keeper of the brothel, stood there grinning stupidly from ear to ear.

'I think you gentlemen are being very ungrateful,' she said coyly, 'very uncharitable.'

Mohsin stood up, appalled by this intrusion.

'Have you been listening at the door?' he demanded.

She waddled into the room, her bangles jingling and jangling on her short, stubby arms. She looked not at all concerned by the fact that she was intruding upon two of the most dangerous men in Mumbai.

'Oh,' she giggled, 'I always listen at the door when business is slow.

Tonight, you would think the men of India have all lost their balls.

Not even our half price hand-job is pulling them in.'

Unfortunate choice of words but darned if I was going to say anything.

I expected Mohsin to grab her by the hair and boot her out.

Instead, his face turning puce, he watched her walk up to his desk and perch an enormous cheek on a corner of it. Backside I mean, not face.

'I just think you are both being rather harsh,' she said.

Had I underestimated this wise, courageous and compassionate woman?

'Please, Sheik,' she said to an obviously aggravated Mohsin, 'just hear me out before you throw me out.

This little fellow has done for you in one stroke what you have not been able to do in a decade. Get rid of Salgaonkar.

He has kept you out of trouble with the police. He has given you a huge business opportunity. He has been a loyal servant to you.'

She looked at Avzal.

'Avzal Bhai, has he ever lied, cheated, stolen from you or disobeyed your orders?'

Avzal shook his head.

I could not believe these men were letting this greasy old lady talk to them in that manner.

'What do you have to fear from him if he leaves?' she asked.

'He has worked for you, run drugs for you, witnessed a shooting, destroyed evidence, planted false evidence, covered up a killing.

If he goes to the police, he'll be the very first one to go into Tihar jail. Don't you agree, Sheik Mohsin?'

He nodded mutely.

'If I were you,' my compassionate champion continued, 'my only question would be who would look after the rickshaws and the delivery business if he leaves?'

I hate leaving questions pending. Invariably it lets people find the wrong answers. So I butted in.

'Madam, as you have brought it up, let me tell you that all I do is look after the rickshaws and make deliveries. I am just the help.

The real boss of that business is Imtiaz here. He takes the orders, makes up the parcels, schedules the deliveries, collects and counts the money.

If anyone should be running the business it should be him.

He's a natural.'

She clapped her hands gleefully.

'Oh, excellent idea. Imtiaz would be a fitting leader of that business. And a real company man too. He deserves a promotion don't you think, Avzal Bhai?'

Again Avzal just nodded.
    Really! Why were they humouring this old crone?

She slowly walked up to me and pulled my head into her giant bosom.

'But most importantly, what has this poor boy asked you in return for all he has done?
    Money, fancy title, corporate expense account? No!
    I understand that you cannot have people leaving the organisation, opening their mouths and potentially become a threat to you.
    But this boy does not want to leave because he wants to set up his own business or compete with you or turn into an informer.
    No. He just wants to go and help his old, ailing parents.
    He wants to help save the family farm and give his dear mother the comfort she deserves in her old age.'

Then, with a definite stoniness of eye, she turned to stare directly at the two men.
    'Isn't that noble of him? Don't you think it creditable? Aren't your parents important to you two?'

Interesting how her voice, so silky at the start, had slowly turned to steel.

Both men were now studiously studying their shoes like two little boys caught stealing mangoes from their neighbour's tree.

'Sheik Mohsin,' she smiled at him, 'to be a big boss one has to have a big heart. Think of how motivating it would be for your employees to know that their boss is wise enough to reward outstanding commitment to the organisation in an outstanding way.

That he is not only a tough disciplinarian but also a generous and gracious human being. A man who can enforce the rules but also, when deserved, bend the rules. A fist of steel inside a velvet glove. Surely that is the hallmark of a great leader?'

I could not believe this lowly brothel keeper was giving the second-ranking executive of Mumbai's most feared organisation a lesson in effective personnel management.

What an insult. Surely now he would order Imtiaz to take her out and behead her?

Thankfully, she released my head from its pendulous prison and walked purposefully up to Sheik Mohsin.

There, horror of horror, she put a hand on his shoulder.

She leaned over him and now, with not an ounce of warmth in her voice, continued the 101 on Enhanced Leadership Skills.

'I think it would greatly benefit your position here, enhance your status in the eyes of your employees if you allowed this fine young man to do what is, after all, the number one duty of every Indian son. To serve his old parents!

Don't you agree Avzal, Mohsin?' she asked them, her voice now as cold and hard as burnished metal.

Neither man looked up at her.

'Yes, Mother,' said Sheik Mohsin.
    'Yes, Bade Mian,' said Avzal.

21

ROLL THE FINAL CREDITS

I skipped down the stairs like a man filled with helium.

I was floating, flying, free!

I no longer worked for the organisation.
  Kalpana would now have me as her partner.
  I would not be dying in a war.

I burst onto the street eager to call Kalpana and tell her everything.

We would go to dinner, celebrate, plan our future.
  Life had never felt more promising.

Everything was resolved...almost.

A deep voice stopped me in my tracks.

'Stop, frog!'

I turned to see Imtiaz standing there, staring at me with a flame in his eyes that sent a shiver through me.

I always knew he'd be the hardest to convince.

As in the cinema, the big-ticket audience – the intelligentsia, the critics, the self-appointed experts and aficionados, judged with their heads.

But the little man, the naive, weak-minded simpleton in the front row judges with his heart.
    And hearts are much harder to sway than heads.

I faced him. There was nowhere left to go.
    Miracle of miracles, I had no more words in me.

He walked up and stood right in front of me, eye to eye, nose to nose.
    'You convinced them. But I warned you, didn't I? I would make sure you got what you deserved.'

He lunged at me suddenly. I closed my eyes.

I waited for the pain of the first stab, but all I felt were two huge arms fold around me and start to squeeze the life out of me.

Really? I thought. Of all the ways to go? Death by body odour?

His animal-like teeth moved towards my quivering ear.

'Thank you,' he whispered.

Then, releasing me as suddenly as he had embraced me, he turned and was gone.

I sighed, took in a gulp of fresh, trouble-free air and reached into my pocket for my phone.

Time to tell Kalpana to get her best party frock on.

THE END.

PUBLISHER'S ADDENDUM

The letter printed here was received by Mr Shah's collaborator, Mr Batliwalla a few days before the first print run of this book.

The writer requests that this letter not be included in the book, as it is intended solely as private correspondence between Mr Batliwalla and himself.

However, upon receiving advice from our legal department, it was decided that the letter should be made available to all those who have followed this story so far.

To not do so, we are advised, could constitute an attempt to hide or distort the full truth.

Therefore, this translation of it is included here:

My Dear Friend,

I am posting this letter at Dubai International airport.

By the time you read it, I will be well on the way to my new home, in my new country.

Surely you did not believe that I could live out the rest of my life tending cattle and milking goats in some godforsaken village in Gujarat?

My father, who by the way is as healthy as a fully intact Brahman bull, would no more tolerate me working on his farm than I could tolerate working 18-hour days in dusty, dung-covered fields.

I have repaid his loans to the bank and hired him 3 full-time labourers to work for him.

He now sits atop his tractor, like a tennis umpire in his high chair, keeping a beady eye on proceedings and calling foul on his workforce every chance he gets.

He is overjoyed to have gone, in one stroke of his son's chequebook, from labourer to lord and master.

No! Mumbai has given me a taste for city life!

I could not live without the hustle, the throb of an urban metropolis.

The shops, restaurants, cafes, bars, theatres.

However, I do not feel it prudent to be seen walking around Mumbai. Who knows when Bade Mian's generosity or Sheik Mohsin's devotion to his mother will expire?

If she were to hear that I was tending to my pleasures rather than tending to my parents, she may well revoke the freedom of passage she gave me.

There is another more compelling reason why I think I best not hang around Mumbai for a while.

You remember that the Saraswati Transport Co. and the rickshaws were all in my name? Well, yesterday I sold all but one of them to the Trimurthy Transport Enterprises for substantially more than the measly price Avzal Bhai paid for it all.

A part of the money has gone towards securing our farm and assuring my parents of a worry-free future, so I have not lied. I have helped them as I said I would.

However, when Avzal Bhai finds out, India will be too small a place for me, so best I look for new opportunities elsewhere.

That is just one reason why I ask that you keep this note private between us.

When I figured out how to end my predicament, the first person I visited was my old flatmate Rashid (Documents and Identities, if you recall) to buy myself a new passport under a new name.

You will understand if I do not reveal it to you.

If you Google 'Golden Visas', you will see several wonderful countries that are only too willing to offer one a new home in exchange wanted for a little 'housekeeping' money.

I have chosen a wonderful land, with plenty of sunshine, long stretches of coastline, laws that are open to personal interpretation and a very accommodating government.

I do not think I shall be at all homesick.

Of course, I am not alone. Kalpana is sitting right beside me in this first-class lounge, sipping champagne and watching me write this.

Our relationship, now free of my job and her responsibilities as a daughter, has taken a wonderful, caring turn.

(No, she is no Deepika, but would Deepika really fall for an irresponsible, carefree, reckless rogue like me? I think not.)

Kalpana is teaching me English.

I am teaching her the importance of living life as you want to, not as others believe you should.

Of taking control before you start taking stock.

As you can imagine, the hardest part of my scheme was to convince her that Bunty deserved an end that was peaceful and pain free. Being a chemistry teacher, she realised that the drug I had managed to get from Salim would, in suitable quantities, give him immediate release from the hell he was suffering.

It's what she had told me she had wanted for him.

I wonder, Shapoorji, do you judge me harshly for my actions?

If Bunty Bhaskar was a German Shepherd or a goldfish, you would applaud me for making sure he did not suffer any further.

Personally, I blame doctors for this ridiculous belief that we must cling onto life, no matter how intolerable or unwanted it may have become.

It's because of this damn oath they take to 'Preserve Life'.

They seem to believe that with their medical degrees they also get a piece of paper that appoints them God's lieutenants with the right to insist on keeping people alive rather than keeping them happy.

If instead they swore to 'Preserve Quality of Life', they may finally find themselves as respected and admired as veterinarians, the only medical profession that understands that 'well-being' is far more important than just 'being'.

I am not at all ashamed of what I did for Bunty, and I know that right now, somewhere up there, he who understood the power of applause, is applauding Kalpana and I for the kindness we have done him.

You may also be wondering how a man with no assets and no savings has managed to fly first class and buy himself a new life?

Obviously that requires substantially more than I got for three rickshaws and an operator's license.

I wonder, Shapoorji, if you have spotted our little subterfuge.

I did carry three bags of clothes up the stairs to the office the day of Kalpana's wardrobe department meeting.
But I did not carry three bags of clothes down the stairs.

After her meeting, Kalpana emptied the cupboard cum safe of the cash in it and filled it with the clothes from the suitcase.
That is why I wanted to make sure the police never saw inside.
An expensive safe filled with cheap clothes? Imagine the questions that would have been raised.

Of course, Bunty's investors are never going to report the theft of their illicit cash hoards; black money that no one is ever supposed to know about.

So, all in all, I think we are home free.

I never lied to you, my friend; I simply told you the truth in a manner that let you interpret it the way you want to.
Isn't that the art of storytelling?

Through my contacts in the organisation, those who change money and arrange for foreign transfers on the black market (Transfers and Exchange Department) that money now sits in an account in our new country.

Fortunately, officials there are as fond of their founding father as Krishna is of Gandhiji.

How at home we shall feel!

Have you ever asked yourself why I went through it all the way I did, all the elaborate scheming and plotting?

Quite simply, I really believed that if I managed to cripple Salgaonkar's organisation, my bosses would have been grateful enough to grant me my request for freedom. How wrong I was.

Without Bade Mian's maternal instinct I would still be riding Saraswati today, delivering our product and working for the organisation.

That evening in Sheik Mohsin's office, fate came down on my side.

That, my friend, was just pure, dumb luck.

But why not just get rid of Talpade myself?

Why go through that entire charade with a drunk drug addict and risk it all going wrong?

As you will appreciate, one organisation member shooting a competitor would have been old news before it even hit the stands. No one would have cared. In fact, the police would probably have been grateful.

To create the groundswell I wanted, the scandal that would lead to action, Bollywood's biggest star had to be the protagonist.

So, I had to make sure that the police believed that there were only two people present in the office that night (I will never ride in the boot of a Padmini Premier again) and they had to find clear evidence of gunfire residue on Bunty's hand.

There is another reason too.

Yes, I am a cheat, a liar, a conman, a drug runner and, for many years, a willing member of a criminal organisation.

But, my friend, believe me, I am not a killer.

True, I helped a man dying in pain to die peacefully.

But I could never have killed a healthy human being in cold blood.

I hope you will believe me, but I will understand if you cannot.

Anyway, enough of the past.

The real purpose of this letter is to tell you that a few days ago, I was sent the printer's galley of our book, and I like what you have done.

Kalpana read it and told me the English was quite OK.

Not as erudite as our own Mr Rushdie, she says, but definitely easier to read.

So thank you.

My one query is about the chapter headings you have chosen, the various ingredients that go into making an Indian movie.

Were you merely trying to reflect my love for the cinema, or are you suggesting that everything I have told you is as invented and unlikely as a Bollywood creation?

I guess, my friend, there are some questions we just have to leave unanswered.

Whether you believe me or not is immaterial, as I have now received the publisher's advance.

You may recall our agreement to split everything 50–50?

Sadly, Kalpana has acquired a taste for first-class comfort, and so, to satisfy our future travel needs, I am now compelled to alter our agreement.

All future royalties have been redirected to my personal account in my new country where I will be holding onto all of them. Needs must, I'm afraid.

But fret not, my friend, you will not go without. Instead of mere money, I plan to give you the most precious gift a man may receive. Unfettered joy!

In a day or two, Imtiaz will deliver Saraswati to your home.

Ride her at will.

Enjoy the thrills she will give you.

Experience the absolute freedom, the exhilaration of a small, three-wheel rickshaw.

But above all, please look after her.

She made everything possible for me, and I will always cherish the times she and I spent together.

Who knows? This exile may not be forever?

Once Bade Mian is gone (she must be 80 if she's a day), Sheik Mohsin runs all Mumbai and Avzal Bhai becomes number two in the organisation, they may forget all about this little episode.

Then, my dear friend, it may be possible for me to come home.
    When I do, we will talk some more, I will feed you more fruit cake and Saraswati and I will drive you through the backstreets and bylanes of our beloved Mumbai again.
    The city where dreams truly can come true.

Until then, with all affection,

your friend,
(and for the last time)
Ricki Shah

ACKNOWLEDGEMENTS

My sincerest gratitude to Roger Barlow, Jim Scully, Juliet Gore, David Butler and Allen Zeleski for their support and encouragement.

And the biggest possible hug to my Lizzie for the cover picture, the proofing and the patience.

Thank you, folks. You helped make it happen.

ABOUT THE AUTHOR

 Shapoor Batliwalla was born in Mumbai India in the 1950s, a halcyon and happy period in Indian history, following the discovery of penicillin and before the advent of the IPL.

He attended six schools in five different countries, although he is adamant this was more an outcome of his family's nomadic existence than any particular scholastic ineptitude.

His only notable achievement through his entire boyhood appears to be that he once got to bowl six balls to Sir Geoff Boycott at the Royal Bangkok Sports Club cricket nets before being advised to take up Scrabble instead.

In his 20s, Mr Batliwalla moved to Australia and, loathing real work of any sort, turned to Australian TV and cinema, playing a string of doctors, lawyers and assorted head-wobbling sub-continentals, minor character roles hardly substantial enough to satisfy stomach or soul.

In time, as his daughters grew vocal enough to demand regular, if not daily, feeding, he was compelled to seek more reliable and regular employment.

This he did by joining a leading Melbourne advertising agency as a copywriter. For the next 40 years, he managed to avoid scrutiny or detection by the simple yet long-heralded advertising tradition of going out to an early lunch and staying there.

Eventually discovered hiding under a desk in 2018, he was summarily despatched into the timeless morass of tedium called retirement, where he attempted to pass the time by writing, for the first time ever, without the misinformation of a brief, the misguidance of a planner or the misdirection of a client.

Mr Batliwalla lives in Melbourne with his two daughters, two sons-in-law, two mortgages, two dogs and two cats.

He has, however, in perhaps the only wise move of his entire life, limited himself to one wife.

CPSIA information can be obtained
at www.ICGtesting.com
Printed in the USA
BVHW030911060521
606646BV00005B/397